P9-DVR-301

LARGE
PRINT
EDITION

RANDOM
HOUSE

MRS. POLLIFAX
AND THE
LION KILLER

DOROTHY GILMAN

Published by Random House Large Print
in association with Ballantine Books
New York 1995

Copyright © 1996 by Dorothy Gilman Butters

All rights reserved under International and Pan-American
Copyright Conventions.
Published in the United States of America
by Random House Large Print
in association with Ballantine Books,
New York, and simultaneously in Canada
by Random House of Canada Limited, Toronto.
Distributed by Random House, Inc., New York.

LIBRARY OF CONGRESS CATALOGING-IN-PUBLICATION DATA
Gilman, Dorothy, 1923–
Mrs. Pollifax and the lion killer / by Dorothy Gilman.
p. (large print) cm.
Sequel to : Mrs. Pollifax pursued.
ISBN 0-679-75872-0
1. Pollifax, Emily (Fictitious character)—Fiction.
2. Intelligence service—United States—Fiction.
3. Women spies—Africa—Fiction.
4. Large type books.   I. Title.
[PS3557.I433M683   1996]
813'.54—dc20   95-37371   CIP

Manufactured in the United States of America
FIRST LARGE PRINT EDITION

This Large Print Book carries the
Seal of Approval of N.A.V.H.

MRS. POLLIFAX AND THE LION KILLER

1

"She mustn't go alone," Cyrus was saying. "Absolutely not—it could be dangerous for Kadi, we both know that."

Mrs. Pollifax looked at her husband, seated on the couch with his left leg heavily encased in plaster and propped on a stool, and she didn't know whether to laugh or to cry. "Cyrus, I can't possibly leave you and go with her," she told him. "Your cast won't be removed for eleven more days, you need help with your crutches, you can't drive, you can't manage cooking or shopping—"

"She mustn't go alone," he repeated firmly. "No matter *what* appeals have come from Ubangiba and young Sammat she mustn't go alone."

Mrs. Pollifax acknowledged this with a sigh. "What's to be done, then? We've practically adopted Kadi—or did she adopt us?" she asked with a smile. "She's spent every weekend with us, when not at art school, and of course I feel responsible, but who can go with her? She's like family."

"Like quicksilver," Cyrus said. "Eager. Curious. Can't have any harm come to her. Those three men . . ."

He didn't finish his sentence but he didn't need to: Mrs. Pollifax had met Kadi Hopkirk eight months ago, literally in a closet, after which the two of them had spent an extraordinary week together that had ended with Carstairs of the CIA whisking them off to Africa, to the country of Ubangiba. It was a relationship that Mrs. Pollifax had assumed would end when she and Kadi parted, but much to her delight it had only begun.

They had known Kadi was an orphan—and why—but they'd been unprepared for the nightmares that had awakened them on a number of the weekends Kadi spent with them: the whimpers, followed by the screams of "No! No!" Kadi had never cared to speak of what she'd seen that day when her parents were executed at their mission station during one of Ubangiba's coups, but over the months of knowing her, and because of those restless sleeps, Mrs. Pollifax and Cyrus had managed to extract from her several small details. There had been three men, Kadi had said reluctantly, not wanting to remember; she had been returning on foot to her father's clinic with a precious bag of salt when she'd heard loud voices, gunfire, and her father's nurse screaming. She'd stood behind a screen of bushes at the edge of the compound to see what was happening, and why Rakia was screaming, and "there were three men," Kadi had said again, tight-lipped.

Cyrus had said, "And did the nurse, Rakia, know who they were?"

Kadi had shaken her head. "They caught and blindfolded her before—before—"

"Then did the three men see *you*?" Cyrus asked.

Kadi had only shrugged, saying, "Right away Rakia and Laraba hid me, and by night the arrangements had all been made to smuggle me out of Ubangiba."

Now Kadi had announced that she had to go back in response to Sammy's call for help. In April, on their brief visit to that country with Carstairs, she had been safe enough; she had been warmly welcomed by old friends but she had been well-protected on that trip. Since then, knowing more, both Mrs. Pollifax and Cyrus had wondered if those three men had survived the brutal reign of President Simoko that had followed the coup, and—if they were still alive—what might happen when Kadi returned again: would they fear being recognized and identified by Kadi, and find it expedient to silence her?

Cyrus interrupted her troubled thoughts to say, "Mrs. Lupacik!"

Jolted, Mrs. Pollifax said, "What? Who?"

"Mrs. Lupacik. Here last month when you had the flu. She could move in, take over."

"But—did you like her, Cyrus? You have to remember I had that horrendous temperature," she reminded him. "I was upstairs in bed and you were in the living room, in the hospital bed, and I scarcely remember *anything*."

Cyrus sighed. "Lightning certainly struck twice! Mrs. Lupacik? Strong as an ox. Puts things where I can't find them, but likable. I could manage. Professional nurse, too, after all. Good cook, and frankly, m'dear, a vacation would do you a world of good. You've lost weight, you're still pale and not at all up to snuff. Between the flu and waiting on me you've tired yourself out."

A vacation, thought Mrs. Pollifax with amusement, *when Sammat is in trouble and has sent out an SOS to Kadi for support and help?*

A troubled African country, Ubangiba, she reflected, small and impoverished. Kadi had grown up there with Sammat, who happened to be the grandson of King Zammat VIII; he had been sent as a boy to her father's mission school, to study and be trained for college abroad. In those days it had not been an impoverished country. It was after the king's death that Ubangiba had been looted and despoiled by coups and atrocities: Sammat's father was the first leader to be assassinated; he had been succeeded by President-for-Life Chinyata, who had done his best to bankrupt the country until he in turn was assassinated in the coup by President-for-Life Simoko. It was during this period that Sammat had been sent off to Yale University, apparently placed on hold by Simoko's government for some future use, when his royal lineage might be exploited or his death adroitly arranged.

His future use had become apparent in April when President-for-Life Simoko had been assassinated. It was from Yale that Sammat had been rescued by Carstairs, with the help of Kadi and Mrs. Pollifax, and during the three days they had all spent in Ubangiba, and even before their departure, the chiefs of the Shambi and Soto tribes had pleaded with Sammat to become *mfumo*, or chieftain, and restore heart to the devastated country. He might be young but he was, after all, the grandson of their beloved King Zammat, and it was Sammat who possessed the sacred royal ring of gold and who had studied abroad such important matters as economics and African agriculture and many other subjects that they hoped might bring a few miracles.

From what they'd learned since April it appeared that Sammat had indeed been producing a few miracles; inflation had fallen, the *gwar* was now worth thirty cents to the U.S. dollar, and he had persuaded the Shambi and the Soto tribes to select representatives to write a constitution that included human rights and elections in three years.

"Except they don't all of them understand what a constitution *means*," Kadi had said, and to Cyrus she had explained, "The Soto are mostly nomads, you know, and only a few of them have had any real education. They've really been quite neglected, so they're very suspicious, and there's a Dickson Zimba among the Soto who *has* had schooling, and is a real troublemaker."

"Ambitious," Cyrus had said, nodding. "There's always one."

"While so many of the Shambi are city people," she'd reminded them. "Merchants, lawyers, teachers, shopkeepers, some of them educated abroad. Sammat is Shambi, too."

In the end, "which no American could possibly understand," Kadi had told them with a grin, "they agreed to take all their disagreements and problems to Sharma, the eldest wise man."

It had been decreed by Sharma, said Kadi, that what the country needed for untangling all the knots and settling the arguments was not a chieftain, a *mfumo*, but a king.

"A king!" Mrs. Pollifax had exclaimed. "Sammat a king? He doesn't want to be a king, does he?"

"No he doesn't, but of course he's the only one

left of the royal line and a king is believed to have magical powers, you see, and is always *respected*."

Mrs. Pollifax had said doubtfully, "Of course he's young—only twenty-three—and I suppose a king has more panache than a mere chieftain."

Cyrus had said with a twinkle, "Being a retired judge I'd certainly be interested in this Sharma's technique in handing down his judicial decisions."

"And you'll be *meeting* him!" Kadi cried triumphantly. "The coronation is one month from now and we're all invited, it'll be great fun, won't it?" She had beamed at them both. "You'll be really impressed by Sharma, he's a medicine man—a diviner—and he must be at least a hundred years old by now. He's the man King Zammat sent for when he was dying. It's Sharma who predicted a reign of evil for ten harvests and counseled the king to have the sacred royal gold ring buried secretly for those ten years. Sharma sees things, he is *wise*."

To forestall any mention of diviners tossing cowrie shells or going into a trance, Mrs. Pollifax had said quickly, "We'll go, won't we, Cyrus? Your cast will be off by then, you may not even need a cane by coronation time!"

"Blessed thought," Cyrus had said, regarding the cast with distaste. "No longer sure I've a leg inside this monstrosity, but if they find one, of course we'll go, m'dear."

That had been ten days ago—a peaceful ten days that had ended last night with Kadi's telephone call from the "Y" in Manhattan, where she lived.

"Who on earth," Cyrus had growled at the ring of the phone. "It's half past midnight, damn it."

At the other end of the line, Kadi was blurting out, "I've just heard from Sammy, Mrs. Pollifax, and he's in *trouble*."

"What do you mean, 'trouble'?" asked Mrs. Pollifax, as yet unprepared to relinquish sleep.

"Rumors, terrible rumors, he says."

"Who is it?" growled Cyrus from his bed.

" 'Rumors'?" and to her husband, in an aside, "It's Kadi."

"He says there may be no coronation," Kadi continued in a rush of words. "He may not even be able to remain a *mfumo*—a chieftain—because someone's been circulating terrible rumors about him—*ominous*, he called them, and the people are growing uneasy too. . . . You remember Joseph . . . he's Sammy's assistant now, and he's not been able to learn anything, or the World Aid people, either."

"But learn what?"

"Learn who is behind the rumors," Kadi said impatiently, and then, with suspicion, "Have you been asleep? Have I waked you up?"

Mrs. Pollifax smiled at Cyrus. "Has she waked us up?"

"Yes!" roared Cyrus. "Ask her why."

"Oh I'm sorry," Kadi said earnestly. "Truly I am, it's just that—"

"Kadi," said Mrs. Pollifax firmly, "just tell us what's the matter. *Clearly*."

In a sobered voice Kadi said, "He sounded desperate. It all began nine days ago and he's not wanted to tell me. He says he's stuck in the capital where no one tells him anything but that I know the villagers, they'd talk to me if I could only come and find out what's behind this. He suddenly can't trust *anyone*."

"But what rumors?" asked Mrs. Pollifax reasonably.

"I don't know," she cried. "He said, 'but there is more, Kadi, much more—' and then we were cut off. I have to go back and help, I must. You understand, don't you?"

Mrs. Pollifax understood Kadi's loyalties, but not the rumors, and it was becoming obvious that Kadi was much too upset to be coherent. "Kadi," she said, "I hear you and I suggest two things: go to bed and get what sleep you can, and then call Sammat in the morning to learn *exactly* what he meant by rumors, and by his saying 'there's more, much more' before you were cut off."

Kadi said anxiously, "Maybe we weren't cut off, maybe someone was listening. To hear Sammy sound as he did scares me, it really scares me."

"All the more reason to wait until tomorrow," Mrs. Pollifax told her calmly. "At eight o'clock in the morning it will be four o'clock in the afternoon in Ubangiba." Or so she thought after doing time zones quickly in her head. Realizing that it was already Friday she added, "I'll meet the six o'clock train today as usual, and we'll talk."

It was after she put down the phone that Cyrus said for the first time, "She can't—*mustn't*—go alone."

Mrs. Pollifax, glancing now at her watch, said, "Kadi's train is due in ten minutes, Cyrus, I've got to go."

He nodded. "And I'll put in a call to Mrs. Lupacik while you're fetching Kadi. See if she's free to move in for a week."

"Oh, Cyrus . . ."

"Yes, m'dear, but we've become surrogate parents and I think her true parents would want this and be glad for it."

Driving to the railroad station, Mrs. Pollifax admitted to herself privately that accompanying Kadi to Africa would normally be delightful, but she could also concede that Cyrus was right: she was still feeling depleted and convalescent from the flu. *I even* feel *pale,* she thought ruefully. It had seemed quite unfair, after faithfully taking a preventative flu shot in the fall, to be felled by a new strain. "Possibly next year's virus," her doctor had said dryly. "Can't explain it otherwise." Now she realized how tiring the trip would be if she went: the two long flights by plane, New York to Paris and then Paris to Ubangiba. On the other hand, she knew that she could never forgive herself if harm came to Kadi and at the same time she remembered there would be sunshine in Ubangiba, and warmth. After a dark and difficult January, and Cyrus's fall on the ice, a week in the sunshine could be therapeutic.

Kadi was waiting at the railroad station when Mrs. Pollifax arrived, and she noted that with each passing weekend Kadi looked a shade less waiflike. It was doubtful that clothes would ever interest her: what mattered to Kadi were her woodcarving, paintings, and friends but today she looked surprisingly trim in black stockings, black shoes, and a beige trench coat, although Mrs. Pollifax noted with amusement the smudge of Alizarin Crimson on one sleeve of her coat, and a torn cuff on the other sleeve. Kadi was small, with a rather plain, fine-boned face and huge eyes, green and thickly lashed. Her brown hair was still slashed with indifference when it reached her shoulders but it was her eyes and an aura of eagerness that drew people's glances. She was different, with an endearing oddness.

Definitely, thought Mrs. Pollifax, *this child has experienced enough horror in her nineteen years of life, and of course I must go.* "How was school?" she asked as Kadi climbed into the car.

"Fine, until Sammy's call last night. How's Cyrus?"

"Bored," said Mrs. Pollifax, maneuvering the car out of its parking space and heading for Maple Lane. "He's tired of reading and has been dipping heavily into soap operas. He'll be delighted to see you."

Kadi said shyly, "Does he disapprove of my leaving school to go for a week or two to Ubangiba? Oh Emmyreed, you understand, don't you?"

Emmyreed . . . That week in April of name changes and disguises! Kadi had worked hard to call her Emmy Reed at Willie's Traveling Amusement Shows, and then she had begun teasingly running the two words together into Emmyreed. Habits acquired in times of danger were not easily exorcised and Kadi reverted frequently.

"We'll talk about it once we're home," Mrs. Pollifax told her with a smile. "And there's pot roast for dinner."

At dinner Kadi said, "It took hours, but I got through to Sammy this afternoon. To tell him that I'm going to do everything I can to get to Ubangi-ba." Her face was somber. "He wouldn't say much, but he said—he said the rumors about him have something to do with witchcraft."

Cyrus gave Mrs. Pollifax an amused glance but she was not amused; she was remembering the beat of talking drums in the dark of night last April, sending news of what had happened on that eventful day, and she was remembering Kadi's serious talk of the medicine men whom her doctor-father had known and respected. He had made friends with many of them and had often used their remedies, Kadi said. Because, she had explained, they were healing people in Africa long before America was discovered. "They *watched*, you see."

"Watched?" Mrs. Pollifax had repeated.

"Yes, they'd see an animal bitten by a poisonous snake and it would run to eat the leaves of a certain plant that caused it to vomit up the poison, and the animal lived. So the village medicine men began making a paste of those same leaves and saved *people*. Centuries ago."

This was the side of Kadi—half-African, half-American—that intrigued Mrs. Pollifax, but she did not underestimate for a moment what Kadi was saying now; Africa's culture was ancient, and ancient beliefs might be hidden but they were not easily exorcised. Witchcraft was serious.

"You have your art classes," Cyrus reminded her gently.

"Yes, but you have to remember I was born in Ubangiba," she said earnestly. "Fourteen years of my life I lived there and it's more home to me, still, than New York. Sammy and I are like brother and sister, and when a person needs help who else is there to want nearby? He *trusts* me, I can find out things for him. I grew up in a village, I know the people and they know me, and it's in the villages that rumors start. Sammy lives in the capital now, in Languka. He knows *I* will be frank and not protect him from what people are saying."

Mrs. Pollifax smiled. She wouldn't, of course; she and Sammat had shared too many scorpion hunts and childhood games for Kadi to think of him as a potential king.

The telephone rang and Mrs. Pollifax looked at Cyrus inquiringly.

"Mrs. Lupacik," he said.

Mrs. Pollifax rose and said, "Hello?" and then carried the phone to Cyrus. "Mrs. Lupacik."

Cyrus answered and listened, nodded and said, "Thank you—bless you for that, I'll call you back in half an hour."

Hanging up he said to Kadi, "But you're not to

go alone, Kadi." And to Mrs. Pollifax, smiling, he said, "Mrs. Lupacik is free, and happy to take over while you're gone."

"You mean—" Kadi looked radiant. "You mean Emmyreed will come with me?"

Seeing their faces she gave a deep sigh of relief. "Oh I'm so glad, I can't tell you how glad that makes me feel." Turning to Mrs. Pollifax she said, "Sammy's last words on the phone today, Emmyreed—I nearly cried—he said, 'Please— *kàm kwík kwík, bo*.' " To Cyrus she explained, "We used to talk pidgin English a lot. I think someone may have been listening in on the phone, or in the same room with him."

"What does it mean?" he asked.

She said soberly, "It means 'come quickly, quickly, friend.' "

2

It was high noon on Monday, three days later, when the plane began its descent over Ubangiba, the smallest and possibly the poorest sub-Saharan country on the continent. First came the desert, she remembered—Soto country—and flying low the shadow of the plane moved with them across the scrub and sand, darkening it like a great flying vulture. The monotony of sand and goats was presently replaced by greening fields, clusters of thatched conical huts, a network of red clay roads, a suburb of square cement bungalows, and then they were flying over the capital of Languka, with its two incongruous white palaces rising above the crowded alleys and flat, dung-colored buildings: a city that had endured riots, massacres, hunger, and decay.

It had been April when Mrs. Pollifax had flown in and out of a deserted airfield; now it was late

January and she peered from the window as they landed, hoping to see signs of change. At once she saw one small difference: a cargo plane stood near the terminal building and was being unloaded by men in overalls; three huge crates sat in the sun, and what looked to be a backhoe was being driven down a ramp.

"Machinery!" breathed Kadi, looking over Mrs. Pollifax's shoulder. "Sammy had such hopes they could afford a backhoe. It must be for opening up the coal mine in the south the geologists found. I just hope they've enough gas to run it!"

A worry about gasoline seemed a strange comment until Mrs. Pollifax remembered that President-for-Life Simoko had bankrupted the country by designing a second palace to outshine the palace that former President-for Life Chinyata had built. Simoko had also cultivated a taste for caviar, quail, and fine, imported wines, and for hoarding gold bullion under his bed. The autopsy that Carstairs had insisted upon in April had proven it was Simoko's caviar that had been poisoned, which was perhaps justice of a sort in a country where his people were starving. Presumably his hoarded gold was paying for the backhoe.

"And look—there's Sammy!" cried Kadi.

Whether he had come to inspect the backhoe or to meet them was not evident until he left the group at the cargo plane to stride across the tarmac toward them. Sammat at least had not changed. He wore a crisp white shirt, open at the throat, that heightened the rich dark color of his skin; his was a strong face, the features well-cut with intelligent eyes under a slash of black brows, and young as he was, and as teasing as he might be with Kadi, there was a natural grace and dignity about him that made one aware of his being the descendant of African kings. He was not in any regal costume today, however; he wore knee-length khaki shorts, high socks, and sneakers. The only sign of his being special was the uniformed guard who walked at his side, and whom she recognized as Joseph. One did, after all, recognize a man who had saved all their lives as Joseph had done in April, but it was obvious that he was no longer a palace servant; his uniform was well-cut and he wore a gun in a holster at his belt.

"Kadi!" shouted Sammat, and after they descended from the plane, he gave her a very American hug and then turned to Mrs. Pollifax, beaming, and hugged her, too. "Friend Pollifax," he said, "welcome back."

Joseph, smiling shyly, reached for her hand, and remembering the traditional handshake, Mrs. Pollifax shook it, clapped her own hands three times, shook his hand a second time, and clapped again.

"*Moni,* Miss Hopkirk," he said, turning to Kadi, and they repeated the greeting.

"You see what has come for us as well as you?" said Sammat, pointing to the cargo plane. "On Thursday digging begins in the south. We've had more tests made and it's anthracite—*good* coal!"

Kadi said teasingly, "But Sammy, future kings aren't supposed to wear shorts and be at the airport watching a backhoe come in, and meeting a pair of *mzungu.*"

Sammat, taking this seriously, straightened his broad shoulders and in that instant Mrs. Pollifax felt that all the kings preceding him through the centuries might be invisible but were nevertheless present beside him. "If I still become king," he said firmly, and Mrs. Pollifax noted the *if,* "I will be a *different* sort of king, I will be accessible. My country needs change."

Joseph nodded. "*Yanga mfumo* go everywhere, he spare none of us." His clipped words reminded Mrs. Pollifax that Ubangiba's first language was English, but British taught.

"Come, let's go," said Sammat, and led them through the shadowed terminal, with a friendly nod to the officers manning Passport and Customs, and out into the bright sun again. A crowd of people waited behind ropes to meet passengers, or simply to experience the twice-weekly plane from across

the ocean: barefooted women in turbans and multi-
colored wrapped skirts as well as women in cotton
skirts, blouses and sandals, the men less colorful in
shorts or slacks and T-shirts. They eyed the passengers with a variety of expressions: envy, awe, astonishment, or amusement. The crowd parted to
allow them through and Mrs. Pollifax thought that
a few, recognizing Sammat, looked startled and uncertain whether to smile or frown.

Pointing to a dusty four-door sedan—President
Simoko's limousines appeared to have been ban-
ished—Sammat had just opened the rear door for
them when a Land Rover came speeding up the
road from the city, blowing its horn with something
like hysteria, clouds of dust following it. Close to
Sammat and his party the Land Rover swerved,
came to a stop, and two of the policemen standing
behind the driver jumped out, shouting, *"Yanga
mfumo! Ngoozi!"*

Sammy gasped. "Another? *Again?*"

Kadi stiffened.

"What's he saying?" asked Mrs. Pollifax.

"He says something terrible's happened."

"Inde, inde," the man said, and resorting to English, "Behind the Bang-Bang Snack Bar, next to
World Aid office!"

Sammat turned to Joseph. "Take Kadi and Mrs.
Pollifax to—no, forget it, no time," and jumping
into the front seat of the car he started up the

engine. Since the door was already open Mrs. Pollifax slid into the rear seat, Kadi behind her, and following the police in the Land Rover they sped down the boulevard that led straight as an arrow to the Simoko palace.

"What is it, Sammy?" asked Kadi.

"Nothing you must see," he said over his shoulder, "but what I *must* see before delivering you to your room. Hold on!"

The boulevard was familiar to Mrs. Pollifax. Many of the walls of the villas that in April had been pockmarked with bullet holes had been mended, and at intervals a worker could be seen slapping on whitewash, half-covered with it himself, and ghostlike. Only one car passed them but the road was not empty: a woman herded a line of goats along its edge; bicycles swerved to give them the right of way; a group of boys in Boy Scout uniforms waved cheerfully. The walls ended and the native market lay ahead, with its bright ragged awnings and stalls, but strangely deserted in the noon sun until Mrs. Pollifax saw why: there had been an exodus across the boulevard, and the crowd from the marketplace had gathered under the neon sign of the Bang-Bang Snack Bar.

Sammat stopped at the edge of the crowd, his brakes squealing in protest. To one of the police in the Land Rover he called, "Show me," and to the other he murmured inaudible instructions. To Kadi and Mrs. Pollifax he said, "Please—stay in the car. This is official."

As he strode away, Kadi sniffed. "I must say, Sammy's getting awfully stuffy now that he's *mfumo*."

"If it's something horrid, I'd call him gallant," pointed out Mrs. Pollifax, and saw that one of the policemen had been posted beside their car. Obviously Sammat had ordered him here; they were not to get out.

Kadi was furiously digging through her knapsack; Mrs. Pollifax looked around appraisingly. Sammat and the policeman had disappeared down a shadowed alley, she could see this through interstices in the crowd. In front of her stood the Bang-Bang Snack Bar, very modern, but adjoining a shabby storefront with the sign WORLD AID. On the other side, separated by the alley, rose a high, crumbling mud wall with a padlocked wooden gate. Over this gate hung a sign that read BIKES SOLD CHEEP. RING BELL. A bicycle was locked to the gate with a chain, its paint faded, one tire flat.

Curious, Mrs. Pollifax leaned out of the open window and tried to discern words in the mumble of voices that rose and fell in waves, sometimes audible, sometimes not. One word seemed to be repeated over and over. *"Mkambo?"* and *"Inde! Mkambo!"* accompanied by a wail, obviously of mourning. *The name of a person, perhaps,* thought

Mrs. Pollifax, and then she saw Sammat emerge from the alley between the buildings and he looked shaken and suddenly very tired. He spoke briefly to several people in the crowd and then returned to the car.

Kadi said angrily, "Sammy, what—" but Mrs. Pollifax gave her a warning nudge and shook her head.

"Later," she whispered. "Wait."

Sammat took his place behind the wheel, backed, turned, and headed down the boulevard toward the bizarre white palace glittering in the sun. They entered the drive, lined with brilliant bougainvillea, and now Mrs. Pollifax saw the changes that Sammat had brought to Languka, for the entrance fairly bristled with small, upright wooden signs, each one in English, with line drawings for those who could not read. The largest read HOSPITAL (a stick figure sitting up in bed); followed by EMERGENCY ROOM TO LEFT (arrow, and a man on a stretcher); MATERNITY CLINIC (very pregnant woman); TEACHING HOSPITAL (arrow to right); and a more modest sign, with arrows: EXPERIMENTAL FARM, AGRICULTURE CENTER (a green leaf and a chicken).

So he had really turned one of the two palaces into the hospital he'd envisioned, and Mrs. Pollifax felt glad for Sammat, as well as impressed, at least until he stopped the car at the entrance and turned to them with eyes that looked as if he'd glimpsed Hell.

Mrs. Pollifax said gently, "What happened back there, Sammat?"

Tight-lipped, he said, "A murder, but—" He stopped. "Later," he said flatly, and opened the car door and slid out. "Please, you've had a long trip. We've prepared a room for you at the top of the palace but, if you prefer, you can later move to the World Aid dormitories."

He gave them a small, twisted smile. "We can't talk now, I'll show you to your room but then I must leave you and speak to Dr. Merrick, and also meet with Chief Inspector Banda."

About the murder, of course, thought Mrs. Pollifax, and now she was remembering Sammat's "Again? *Another?*" and she wondered.

As Sammat walked around the car to retrieve their luggage Kadi said sadly, "I don't feel—very *welcomed.*"

Mrs. Pollifax felt her hurt and reached for her hand and squeezed it. "I think we've arrived at a very difficult time, Kadi. Sammat is a very worried young man and that's why we're here, remember? Let him choose his time to talk."

Kadi sighed. "He's so *polite.*"

"We'll be polite, too," Mrs. Pollifax told her with a smile.

Sammat, bags in hand, gave Kadi a warmer

smile. "I'm glad you're here, really glad, Kadi, and if you want to see Rakia she's head nurse now in our emergency room."

Kadi said with a gasp, "Here, in the palace? Then I can see her this afternoon! How *wonderful.*"

To Mrs. Pollifax Sammat said politely, "And you must visit our greenhouses later, and see the experimental farm; we've been having really good luck growing red-bulb onions as a crop."

Mrs. Pollifax brightened at this; greenhouses were familiar, and just now, after flying over two continents to reach a third, she felt a passionate need for the familiar. Her geraniums at home blossomed nearly all year in her greenhouse, well-nourished by her conversations with them, and while she wasn't sure that she could feel quite the same about red-bulb onions it would nevertheless be reassuring to see *something* growing out of the earth. "I'd like that," she told him, and as they walked into the palace she stopped in surprise.

What had last year been a huge and empty marble-floored hall was filled with people now. On benches lining one wall the local Ubangibans waited for treatment in the clinic, the women holding babies, the men stoic and silent. A black man in a white jacket crossed the hall, followed by a white man in a black jacket. A young woman sat at a desk as small boys raced around her and then back to their mothers or fathers again.

Sammat said wryly, "You see how resourceful we've had to be," and he pointed to the balcony at the top of the main staircase from which ropes were suspended, knotted and secured to stretchers waiting on the floor. "We have no elevator, and while the clinic and the emergency room are down here, the operating room is on the second floor."

"Very ingenious," murmured Mrs. Pollifax as they began climbing the broad staircase, only to be faced with another set of stairs to the third floor. The room that she and Kadi were to share was small and plain—"no private bath, but there's one at the end of the hall," Sammat said. "Joseph will bring your suitcases."

Depositing their carry-on bags he added, "You'll both want to rest, we'll have dinner together. Early, at five. In the meantime," he said with a rueful smile, "welcome to Ubangiba."

When he had gone Kadi said, "Well, I'm not going to rest, not if Rakia's downstairs. She'll be busy so I'll just say hello. You don't mind?" she asked anxiously. "Unless you want to come, too?"

It occurred to Mrs. Pollifax that the last thing she wanted was to become Kadi's shadow, or an obligation. Nor did she want to rest, either. Jet lag had promoted an edgy restlessness in her and what she wanted after the long plane flight was to connect with her surroundings. She said vaguely, "Oh

I might take a short walk. Just to see a little of the town."

"Then wear a hat, the sun can be ferocious," Kadi reminded her. "Don't go far, I really won't be long."

When she had gone Mrs. Pollifax opened her carry-on bag and brought out her thinnest dress, a pair of sandals, and a very crushed straw hat. Changing into the dress and persuading the hat into shape again she left the room. She had noticed on their drive down the boulevard a hand-lettered sign announcing THE BANK OF UBANGIBA, and she thought this a sensible time to change American money into Ubangiban *gwar.* Descending the two staircases she walked out into the heat of the afternoon and crossed the boulevard to the shady side.

At once there were people, shops and stalls to capture her interest, and Mrs. Pollifax enjoyed people. She passed shops selling jewelry, secondhand furniture and leather shoes in rainbow colors, and when she paused at an outdoor stall heaped with beadwork the salesman looked up, saw Mrs. Pollifax and gave her a big smile showing white teeth filed to a point. Farther along the boulevard was a sign promising DRESSES STRAIGHT FROM LONDON, and at the corner she was intrigued by a man seated on a strip of canvas and surrounded by jars of what looked to be dried snakes and baskets full of strange-looking herbs.

Reaching the bank Mrs. Pollifax entered, showed her passport, asked for an exchange of currency, and waited patiently while two clerks and the manager struggled over a computer, ultimately abandoning it to figure the rate of exchange on an abacus. Once this transaction was completed she thanked them and left, clutching a wad of *gwar* that she stuffed into her purse, and continued up the boulevard. She thought that she might walk as far as the Bang-Bang Snack Bar and the gate next to it with its sign BIKES SOLD CHEEP. She remembered both as being not far, and side by side, and in the meantime she was pleased at being out in the world again. She received a few timid smiles from passersby, as well as a number of curious glances, but what most of all interested her was the fact that, in the absence of cars, so many citizens of Languka rode past her on bicycles.

Seeing a middle-aged man in business suit, white shirt and tie ride past her with a briefcase slung over the handlebars, Mrs. Pollifax decided that she would like to have a bicycle, too. It was true that except for one insane ride downhill in a recent adventure she had not ridden a bicycle since she was Kadi's age, but she thought that with a little practice she could easily recapture the technique. *When in Rome, do as the Romans do,* she reminded herself piously, and to have her own means of transportation in a city short of gasoline and cars, the idea had a distinct appeal.

With resolution she reached the gate of the bicycle shop and stood back to read again its stern instructions: RING BELL. Through a crack in the wooden boards of the gate she could see a square earthen compound, its opposite wall formed by a small house with a door. To her left a few bicycles leaned against the wall in the sun; to her right a long and ragged awning shaded a forest of old bikes. She grasped the rope and pulled it, wincing at a clamor so loud that her ears were ringing after it stilled. It produced a man, however, a giant of a man who emerged from among the bicycles, big-shouldered and broad-faced, with a shaven black head that gleamed like polished mahogany. He was not young: he wore shabby jeans and looked disgruntled, even hostile, as he opened the gate a few inches and stared at her. "Yayezz?"

For just a moment Mrs. Pollifax thought of retreat: there was a terrible scar running from his cheekbone to his jaw, knotted and twisted like a scarlet rope; this and the shaved head, the hostile gaze, the absence of any other people beyond the gate gave her pause until, refusing to be afraid, she told him, "I have come for a bicycle."

"You?"

"Me."

He studied her with suspicion, scowled, hesitated and then grudgingly opened the gate, saying crossly, "Come in, come in. What for you wish a bike?"

"Don't you want to sell one?"

The gate closed behind them; he loomed above her, taller even than Cyrus and massively built. With hands on his hips he looked down at her and said scornfully, "I see you at airport this morning with *Mfumo* Sammat. My bikes be old, used and used and used. No pretty bikes here for a *mzungu.*"

She said tartly, "Did I ask for a pretty new bike?"

"But you come to me, Moses, why? *Ku-zonda?*"

She looked at him with exasperation. "I've no idea what *kuzonda* means, what I want is a bike, and I must say, you're a very strange salesman. Why do I want a bike? To be free, of course, to go by myself where I choose. *Free.*"

"Free," he repeated, seeming to taste the word as he stared at her, and then with a shrug, "Go look, then, bikes along the wall be for selling." He pointed, not moving.

Feeling quite cross at his lack of hospitality, and rather like a trespasser, she gingerly approached the dozen bicycles leaning against the wall, but found only four of them designed for a woman wearing a skirt. After looking each one over she mounted a large and very ancient one, put her feet to the pedals, and rode in a circle around the man, swaying wildly. He watched without expression as she returned the bicycle to the wall, but when she mounted a second one he retreated to a bench to watch, possibly to avoid being hit. There he sat and observed her as she tried out the remaining bicycles. At last, pointing to the second one she made her decision. "This green one. The seat's too high for me—you can adjust that, can't you?—but the brakes are good, and the bell rings. How much?"

He shrugged. "Two hundred *gwar*."

She said accusingly, "That sounds to me like forty U.S. dollars!"

"Yayezz," he drawled.

She replied to this dryly, "And what would the price be for someone who did *not* get off a plane this morning to be met by a future king?"

A faint smile hinted at appreciation of this counterthrust. "Fifty, maybe eighty *gwar*," he told her, and waited to see what she would say to this.

Definitely he was playing a game with her and a dozen retorts came to her mind, but the sun was hot as a cauldron across her shoulders and she felt suddenly weak, as if all of her energy was being siphoned out of her. Worse, a feeling of abrupt and violent alienation swept over her. Panic had struck, so that suddenly she had no idea what she was doing here, or why she wanted a bicycle, or why she was speaking to this unfriendly scarred man in this alien country, or why she had ever left Cyrus, and the utter futility of her coming to Ubangiba overwhelmed her. She grasped the pole of the awning and clung to it, willing herself not to faint, while the man stood and watched her, puzzled, until he said politely, "You be sick?"

She gazed at him without comprehension, his voice thundering in her ears, and then quite suddenly a cloud of darkness obscured him and her surroundings, the earth tilted sideways and she had time only to gasp before she slumped to the ground.

When she opened her eyes she was lying on the bench in the shade and this strange giant of a man was fanning her with a newspaper.

"Breathe," he told her sternly.

"I *am* breathing."

"Breathe *deep*."

As she struggled to sit up he helped her, nodding. "Sit," he said, and went into the little house and returned with a cup of water. "Please," he said, handing her both a cup and a handkerchief. When she hesitated he added, "Water be boiled."

She grasped the cup and managed a feeble smile. "Thank you. I'm sorry. I've never fainted before— *never*—it's just that I was sick last month with the flu, and my husband had fallen on the ice and broken his leg, and—and I've come so *far*. I never *never* should have come!"

He said gruffly, "But there is no need to apologize, I know what it is like to faint, I know what it is like to be sick."

Startled, she said accusingly, "Suddenly now you've changed how you talk, you just spoke perfect English, admit it!"

He shrugged. "I thought you came to my shop to—but I remember now you were here before, weren't you? Last year. You came with the police and brought *Mfumo* Sammat back to us, and with you was Dr. Hopkirk's daughter."

She nodded. "Yes, I was here. Did you know Kadi's father?"

"Long ago, yes. Everyone knew Dr. Hopkirk."

"He was murdered when, five years ago? Six?"

"So I heard, yes."

"Heard?"

He said simply, "I was in prison."

"Oh."

There was a long silence during which neither of them looked at the other, and then she glanced at his scarred face and asked, "How long in prison?"

He held up seven fingers. "Until last year, when *Mfumo* Sammat came back and freed us."

He had captured her full attention now. "But that's horrible, seven years."

His hand moved to touch the thick rope of scar

on his face. "Prison does not teach a man to trust."
His voice was rueful. "The *cha mwai*—the lucky
ones—died early," he said.

"Torture," she murmured, nodding, and remembering an experience of her own in Hong Kong she
reached out and impulsively touched his hand,
withdrawing it quickly lest this affront him.

Turning to look at her he said, "Why *did* you
come to Ubangiba?"

Truth lay between them now and she said with
a sigh, "I had some sort of irrational fear that
Kadi—Dr. Hopkirk's daughter—might be in danger
here and shouldn't come alone."

He thought about this. "You were kind, then, and
wise. Very wise."

"Wise?" she repeated, startled. "What makes
you say that?"

"You came last year with a policeman, didn't
you? Are *you* some kind of police?"

"Oh no," she told him. "That is—" She blew her
nose. "Not exactly."

"Not exactly?"

She shook her head. "Not now, on this visit,"
and when he nodded she said, "You've stopped
pretending suddenly. Who are you?"

"Me? Nobody."

"You've not always mended and sold old bicycles, surely?"

He stretched out his legs in the sunshine, regarding their length with some surprise. He said meditatively, without expression, "Who am I?" He sighed. "Long ago I was a *mwamuaa*, a man; there was a house, a wife, two sons, all dead now. Oh yes I was a man once, I scarcely remember it now."

"But seven years in prison for what reason?"

"It is best to be invisible, why should I tell you?"

"I can't think of any reason why you *should* tell me," she admitted frankly.

"Or any reason why I shouldn't," he acknowledged. "But that was a long time ago, too, when Zammat VIII was king, and I was with the police then. After he died, after his son was assassinated, President Chinyata took power and built the first palace in our country. There was much hunger, and when the hunger riots began—oh, he was angry. Many went to prison, most especially the police. He killed and killed." He shrugged. "Now I am nobody, mending old bicycles, I hide myself away, as anyone must who is a nobody." With an effort he turned to her, brushing aside the past to say, "I am sorry that you come to this country when there is so much trouble—"

"What trouble?" she asked quickly.

Ignoring her question he said, "I would give the bicycle to you but it won't put food on my table. I will sell it to you for one hundred *gwar* if you still want it."

She respected his change of subject and nodded.

"Twenty U.S. dollars is fair," she told him, "and you've been very kind, and I do apologize for suddenly, for suddenly—"

He said in a harsh voice, "You are tired. You are not young. Cry a little and rest. Find a bed and sleep, and then you will fly home, yes?"

Startled, she said, "Home? Oh no, I was quite wrong about that." She added with a faint smile, "And how can I go home when I have just bought a bicycle?"

He nodded and stood up, saying, "I will adjust the seat for you."

She followed in his shadow, and when he put aside his tools, the job finished, she counted one hundred *gwar* into the palm of his huge hand. "I'm Emily Pollifax," she told him, "but you haven't told me your last name."

"Just Moses."

So he trusted no one, even with his full name. Accepting this she was about to climb on the bicycle when he said, "You are strong enough to return?"

She nodded. "I'm not sure I could walk back, but ride, yes."

His eyes narrowing he said, "Do not be too free where you ride. Be watchful."

"*Watchful?*"

He regarded her thoughtfully. "It would be wise. Where there is *imfa—zitatu imfa* now—there will be no pity." He strode to the gate, opened it, and waited for her to go. She wanted to ask him what he meant by no pity and what the words *imfa* and *zitatu* meant, but his face was tight and shuttered again, the sun glancing off the high slant of cheekbones and turning his scar an angry red. She pushed the bike past him to the street and turned to say, "I hope I see you again, Moses."

The gate was half-closed when he said abruptly, "Be watchful," and then, flatly, *"There are no lions in Ubangiba."*

Now that was a non sequitur, she thought, *since everyone knew there were no lions in Ubangiba.* With a wave of her hand she mounted the bike and pedaled rapidly down the boulevard, still out of practice but nursing the assumption that with increased and giddy speed she could maintain equilibrium. With much ringing of the bicycle's bell she succeeded in threading her way among her fellow cyclists, narrowly missing several of them, and overlooking their gasps of alarm she returned successfully to the palace. Here she humbly admitted her need for rest and proceeded to sleep until nearly five o'clock, when Kadi woke her for dinner.

3

F ive of them sat down to early dinner that evening in a tent set up in the garden behind the
hospital's kitchen. Joseph had joined them, followed by a Dr. Merrick. "White medicine man," he
said with a smile as he shook hands with them.
"Surgeon and dispenser of pills."

It was obvious that Sammat was not inclined to
explain or speak of the death he'd seen, or of any
troubles he was experiencing; the conversation became a mixture of shop talk—hospital supplies,
sand fleas, and crop rotation—to which Mrs. Pollifax only half listened. She wondered if Sammat
was sorry now that she and Kadi had arrived and
was realizing how little help they could provide, or
if he simply needed a respite from his worries for
an hour. She was still feeling embarrassed, too,
about fainting at Moses's bicycle shop, and because
of this she questioned just what role she could play

if she was to go around falling over and being laid out on benches.

Their dinner was a modest one of yams, hard-boiled eggs, and stewed chicken, with a bread sauce that resembled a dumpling. When they had begun eating, the sky had been ravished with color but now they were surrounded by night, and with the abrupt setting of the sun at six o'clock an evening chill was stealing into the tent and wrapping itself around her shoulders and ankles. Two candles sputtered on the table, alternately shadowing and illuminating their faces and Mrs. Pollifax, observing each in turn, gained the impression that Joseph did not like Dr. Merrick. *Jealous, perhaps,* she thought, this Joseph who had saved their lives in April, and who no doubt had a proprietary feeling toward this *mfumo* who had promoted him from palace servant to assistant and guard. "My right hand," Sammat had said of Joseph. He was lighter-skinned than Sammat, of medium height and broad-shouldered, with a small head, the face smooth, the flesh drawn taut as a drumhead across high sharp cheekbones; his eyes were small, alert, and intelligent and almost disappeared on the rare occasions when he smiled; a serious man, Joseph. Sammat had said he claimed to be in his forties, but this was a matter of guesswork since he had been born in the shanty-town outside of Languka, where no birth records could prove it, but it was possible; he bore the

marks of a man who had survived that sort of life.
There was a wariness about him, a watchfulness,
and Mrs. Pollifax thought that no one would ever
catch Joseph off guard.

Dr. Merrick, on the other hand, bore the ease and
manner of a man with a conscience who had lived
a privileged life and had resolved to share it with
those less fortunate; he was British, probably forty,
his black hair flecked with gray, thin patrician features, a quick and friendly smile. His talk was of
vaccinations, AIDS, and eventually, the backhoe
that had arrived that morning.

"Yes, the backhoe," Sammat said, and turning to
Kadi and Mrs. Pollifax, "On Thursday we leave at
six A.M. in a cavalcade to see the backhoe make its
first major excavation at the mine. I think you will
find it of interest, it'll be a real celebration. Joseph,
the buses, has the paint dried yet?"

Joseph nodded. "They be ready I *think*. I go see
now." He rose and left, and Dr. Merrick, glancing
at his watch, said, "Time for me to get back to
work, too, but delighted to meet you both. Thanks,
Sammat."

In the silence that followed, Mrs. Pollifax heard
the rhythmic beat of drums in the distance. "Talking drums?" she asked.

Sammat smiled faintly. "Not tonight. What
you're hearing is the Picadilly Popcorn Rock Band.
Very talented! You haven't seen the second palace

yet, it has an auditorium and they're rehearsing there tonight."

"Cool," said Kadi politely, giving Sammat a puzzled glance. "And a cavalcade on Thursday, with a bus?"

"Three buses. Very old," he said ruefully, "but repaired in our new machine shop and painted by the students in the textile class we've begun. The chiefs and the sub-chiefs of the Shambi and Soto will go with us. It's important they be involved, and all the rites are being taken care of tomorrow."

Kadi, turning to Mrs. Pollifax, said, "That means the medicine men will be there making sacrifices to the spirits in the hills so they won't be angry or affronted."

"That would include your friend Sharma, too?" inquired Mrs. Pollifax dryly, and to Sammat, "Will we also meet the Mr. Zimba, whom you described to Kadi as a troublemaker?"

"Dickson Zimba?" Sammat looked startled. "Oh yes, he'll go with us, but troublemaker is really too strong a word." He grinned. "How about gadfly? He's certainly made himself an opposition party. He does have ideas, some of them very good. I can't dislike him, he's had a good solid education at the Church of Scotland mission in the south, and he intends to be a leader of the Soto, but unfortunately he argues every single word in the proposed constitution and he argues *interminably*."

"What sort of man is he?" asked Mrs. Pollifax.

Sammat shrugged. "Not old. About twenty-eight or thirty, and son of one of the sub-chiefs. Ambitious. He's an accountant just now in one of our offices. Quite a firebrand when he makes a speech, otherwise he's—well, the son of a Soto shepherd who has an education, which heaven only knows is what the country needs. The Soto are very proud of him."

"But a bit difficult," agreed Mrs. Pollifax, nodding. "What does he want?"

"I'd say to make trouble," Kadi put in defiantly.

"No, no," Sammat demurred. "He's restless, that's all. He wants change, but we disagree on what's possible just now. He doesn't appreciate the World Aid people being here, for instance. I suspect he wants all white people sent home—Africa for Africans only—but he forgets that our best and most talented people have been killed or been in prison for years and we have to start all over again."

This reminded Mrs. Pollifax of earlier events in her day and what she had wanted translated. From her pocket she brought out the words that she'd written down phonetically on a slip of paper. "Tell me," she said, glancing at it, "what does *ku-zonda* mean?"

"*Ku-zonda?* It means to spy," said Kadi.

So that was who Moses had thought at first that

she was, or might be, this man who guarded even his last name. "Thank you, and there are three more words. The next two are *imfa* and *zitatu*?"

Sammat gave her a quick, sharp glance.

"Those aren't friendly words," Kadi told her. "Who on earth have you been talking to? *Imfa* means death and *zitatu* means three."

Sammat sat still and silent, his eyes probing Mrs. Pollifax's face, but he said nothing.

"Which brings us to the word *mkambo*," she concluded.

"Oh, that's the word for lion," said Kadi, "except of course there are no lions in Ubangiba."

It was becoming monotonous being told this. She lifted her gaze to Sammat and said, "We've come a long way to help, Sammat, and you've avoided explaining what made you desperate enough to ask for it. *Have* there been three deaths—three murders?"

He rose from the table and walked out of the tent, peered right and left into the dark garden and returned to say, "Let's talk in your room."

They walked together back into the palace and up the broad staircase not speaking. They turned left, to confront the second long staircase, and passed the empty surgery, Sammat nodding to a nurse who was closing and locking doors. He said casually, "Tomorrow perhaps Joseph or I can show you around Government House, the smaller palace.

It's where our radio station is located, and the weekly newspaper, and of course the auditorium, and—" His voice trailed away as they reached the door to the guest room and Mrs. Pollifax unlocked it.

Once inside she said, "All right, Sammat, what so shocked you at the Bang-Bang Snack Bar? You spoke of a murder?"

He remained beside the door, and standing there said in a hard voice, "Nine days ago the rumors began, the day after it was announced that I would become king. Dr. Merrick brought me news of the rumor—one of his patients had told him. Dr. Merrick laughed about it at the time."

"What rumor?" asked Kadi.

"That I—I, their *mfumo*, their chief—am a sorcerer."

Kadi looked at him with horror. "A sorcerer? A *sorcerer*?"

He nodded. "It seemed harmless—ridiculous—at first," Sammat said. "I thought perhaps it had something to do with plans to open the coal mine, to make a hole in the earth, to perhaps disturb some shrine we knew nothing about."

To Mrs. Pollifax he said awkwardly, "What I must tell now is difficult—too bizarre for you, Mrs. Pollifax, a *mzungu*—to understand, perhaps, but in Africa there have always been secret societies, most of them for good but some of them very very evil."

"Tell us," she said.

His glance moved to Kadi and he said gently, as if to a child, so that Mrs. Pollifax understood that it was Kadi who concerned him, "You remember Nomsa, Kadi? The woman whom your parents once brought up from the village to look after you when so many people had chicken pox and your parents were busy?"

"Nomsa? Oh God," Kadi said, and covered her face with her hands. "Sammy, don't remind me, she terrified me!"

"Yes, until your parents learned why you were having nightmares and sent her home. What did she threaten you with, Kadi?"

Kadi said shakily, "With the Lion Men of Singida. Except she never told me they were in Tanzania, not here. She said if I once again left the compound, if I didn't behave and obey her, the Lion Men would steal me and hide me in a deep pit, and give me only scraps of food and keep me there until I was old enough to—to go out and *kill* for them."

"In America," commented Mrs. Pollifax, "we have ghosts or bogeymen, but who on earth are the Lion Men of Singida? Are they real or a myth?"

"Real enough, unfortunately. A cult of assassins.

In what is now Tanzania," Sammat said. "Whether they still exist I don't know, but they *did* steal or buy children, and starve and train them, and when someone wanted an enemy killed they went to the sorcerers—the cult of sorcerers called the Lion Men—and paid to have that enemy killed, and the sorcerers produced a child who was sent out in lion skin and mask, with long sharp fingernails to kill. The cult terrorized everyone, and always they left their victims clawed to death, as if by a lion."

"But it never happened *here*," Kadi said.

"That's understood," he said flatly, "but the man found behind the snack bar this morning had been clawed to death."

Kadi gasped. Mrs. Pollifax had begun to fear he was going to say this but it came as a jolt nevertheless, and brought a chill.

Sammat's lips tightened. "The name of the man killed today was Silumo, and this death I saw. Four days ago—this I did not see—a man named Jonas was brought in from shantytown with horrible claw marks all over his body, and Dr. Merrick can tell you that eight days ago, in a village farther south, they showed him a man attacked and killed by what they called 'a wild beast.' "

"Then it's begun here?" said Mrs. Pollifax, frowning. "A secret society like that?"

His voice was grim. "Very neatly timed with rumors that I am a sorcerer . . . The Lion Men were sorcerers and killed in just such a manner."

Appalled, Mrs. Pollifax said, "Then someone is trying—oh, *diabolically*—to connect you with those terrible murders!"

"Oh Sammy," Kadi said in a shocked voice. "Sorcery is *bad* magic. Sorcerers are worst of all— dark and full of death. *Evil.* But why?"

"To destroy me, of course." He placed his hand on the knob of the door and opened it, but before leaving he said bitterly, "It seems it is not enough to bring in World Aid, and make a hospital out of a palace and open schools again, and write a constitution, when a single rumor followed by three deaths can bring such terror to the people they will soon curse me, grandson of King Zammat, and wish me dead."

The door closed behind him and there was a long silence until Mrs. Pollifax said gently, "Kadi?"

"Yes?"

"Does it frighten you? Are you sorry you came?"

"Of course not. You know he asked me to go into the villages—"

"But not alone—*never* alone," Mrs. Pollifax said sternly. "*Ever.* Promise?"

Kadi grinned. "You're saying I'm not much good yet at the karate you've been teaching me?"

"You know what I mean," Mrs. Pollifax said.

Kadi nodded. "I know. But I'm sorry he made me remember Nomsa."

Curious, Mrs. Pollifax asked, "How could Nomsa have known about those Lion Men in a country so far away?"

Kadi shrugged. "We all had battery-powered saucepan radios—cheap and primitive little radios, called that because they looked like saucepans. But news always travels fast in Africa."

As people keep telling me, thought Mrs. Pollifax and she watched Kadi pick up her hairbrush and begin to feverishly brush her hair, as if to banish Nomsa again from memory. Mrs. Pollifax, studying her face, wondered if now might be a time to chance the question she had been waiting to ask. It was risky, and the worst possible moment, and yet . . . She drew a deep breath. "Sometimes it's good to remember the past, Kadi—for *protection*," she told her. "Forgive me if I ask something you've never made clear and that I need to know: did you recognize any of the faces of the three men who came to your father's clinic that day? You said Rakia had been blindfolded, but *you*—"

"No," Kadi said sharply, *"No!"* and she turned away to resume brushing her hair. But seeing Mrs. Pollifax's reflection in the mirror she hesitated, and then, angrily, "All right, I saw one of them. Clearly. As they left. He turned his head and I saw him but it was no one I'd ever seen before."

"And he saw you?"

"Yes," admitted Kadi, "but he didn't say any-thing, he didn't stop, he just followed the other two men down the path."

"Yet one of them knew you were hiding there and watched them leave?"

"Yes, but I was out of the country by night, you know."

Mrs. Pollifax nodded. "Thank you," she said, and picking up her toothbrush she went off down the hall to find the bathroom and brush her teeth, not at all reassured by what Kadi had told her. It didn't seem to occur to Kadi that the man who had looked back and seen her might have told the oth-ers that she was hiding in the tall grass. It was rea-sonable to assume they'd wonder how long she had been standing there, and how much she had seen. . . . For that matter, Mrs. Pollifax was not at all certain that Kadi would remember her promise not to wander off alone: the young were often im-pulsive. *A gun,* she thought; Kadi was a novice at karate, but every night at the carnival she had shot down ten moving ducks with a BB gun at Pogo's rifle range; she was an expert markswoman.

Kadi must have a gun, she decided, and she fell asleep wondering how to find a gun for her in a country where two dictators had long ago banned them out of fear of revolution.

4

"Try the black market," Dr. Merrick told her in the morning, looking amused.

"Oh dear, must I?"

"Yes and you'll pay a pretty price for one. You know the public market on the right side of the boulevard, as you drive in from the airport?"

She nodded. "Across from the Bang-Bang Snack Bar?"

"Yes. Stroll around behind it—discreetly—and you'll find an ex-mercenary they call Jim-Jim. Lebanese or Egyptian, who knows? But you mustn't go alone, of course, ask Joseph to go with you."

Mrs. Pollifax thanked him, and once he had disappeared up the staircase into the surgery she placed her wide-brimmed hat on her head, and with no intention of enlisting Joseph, she mounted her bicycle and set out to find Jim-Jim. It was now or never, she felt, since Sammat had promised to

show them the other palace—the smaller one—
after lunch, and Kadi was lurking in the infirmary,
hoping for a few minutes to interview a busy Rakia
about the rumors, once the nurse took a break.

The boulevard was as usual alive with people,
but it slanted just a little uphill so that Mrs. Pollifax was huffing and puffing when she reached the
public market. Dismounting and wheeling her bicycle, she walked around looking over the infinite variety of wares on display: sacks of charcoal and
millet, a stand selling rolled tobacco leaves, an entire aisle given over to cages of live chickens, a cu-
bicle selling dishes, bowls, mirrors, scissors, and
brooms. She winced a little at the sight of dead
mice for sale, admired the fresh pumpkin leaves,
yams, and peanuts, and particularly the woven baskets of all shapes and sizes.

While reconnoitering, so to speak, she identified
the only two booths with a narrow space separating
them, thus forming an exit through which, presumably, she could reach what lay behind the market. It
was rather difficult to negotiate with her bicycle,
but once through it she arrived in a compound
bearing a single acacia tree around which a number
of rascally looking young men loitered. There were
also a thatched hut and a ragged army tent of considerable size, its flaps open to the sun. The young
men stopped talking at sight of her; she bowed politely and headed for the tent.

"Mr. Jim-Jim?" she called, peering inside.

He appeared behind her, startling her, a tall and unsavory-looking man with a patch over one eye and a band of red cloth tied around his head.

"So," he said, looking startled himself. "Has a white *mzungu* lost her way? The market," he said, pointing a stained finger, "is that way. You think maybe a ladies' room back here?"

She said pleasantly, "Not at all, I hear that you sell guns."

He looked pained. "Now who told you that? And what would someone like yourself want with such a thing?" He smiled at the young natives under the tree, and they laughed appreciatively.

Mrs. Pollifax murmured, "Comedian," and turned and walked into the tent.

"Hey!" he shouted, but it was too late.

She had already seen the trestle table fashioned out of rough boarding, with its samples laid out on display. An exit had been cut into the rear of the tent, a truck parked just behind it, no doubt for a quick getaway. She saw cartons of English cigarettes and of Jack Daniel's whiskey, cases of food, and several guns half-hidden behind a case of Jamaican rum. She leaned her bicycle against a tent pole, pushed aside the case of rum, and glanced over the selection. "Well, well," she said, "an M-1 carbine, a Beretta submachine gun, a Sten . . . but what I want is a pistol, do you have a pistol in your truck?" She pointed to the door in the canvas.

His one eye was gray and expressionless but both of his eyebrows were scowling. He looked baffled. "What the hell kind of lady know Stens and Berettas, I ask you? Not ladylike."

"I'm not at all ladylike," she told him, "and do you have a pistol?"

"They cost plenty."

"I'll judge that when I see them," she said tartly.

He walked to the truck behind the tent and came back with a handful of pistols to dump on the table. Only one or two of them looked new; she thought they must have been smuggled into Ubangiba through many other countries and black markets, and used in many a war and revolution. There was an M-52, a Browning Hi Power pistol, and a much newer looking Makarov 9mm.

"Have you ammunition for this?" she asked, pointing to the Makarov. When he nodded she said, "Then load it for me, please, I'd like to make sure it works."

He swore volubly, reached under the table and giving her reproachful, angry glances he slipped in the cartridge and handed it to her. It would be excellent for Kadi, she decided, only a little over six inches in length and light in weight. Pointing it at the ceiling of the tent she pulled the trigger, which brought a curse from Jim-Jim.

"You make holes in my tent? You pay for that plenty!"

"Ah, but how fortunate that I didn't shoot *you*," she pointed out. "How much does this cost?"

"Fifteen thousand *gwar*!" he told her. "Or," he added, with a shrewd glance at her purse, "five hundred U.S."

"I'll pay three hundred fifty in U.S. traveler's checks," she told him.

He looked horrified. "Traveling checks? My God no. Cash only!"

"How much cash?"

The traditional battle of wills called bargaining began, with Mrs. Pollifax inhibited by the fact that she had only three hundred U.S. dollars with her for the purchase. They settled at last on three thousand *gwar* and three hundred U.S., which she considered a triumph since it added up to only four hundred dollars. She unloaded the pistol, placed it and the package of cartridges in her purse, and counted out the money to him.

"If you speak of this . . ." he said threateningly.

"Why on earth would I do that?" she told him, and assuring him that it had been a pleasure to meet him she walked out of the tent with her pistol and her bicycle.

She had drawn more attention than anticipated, however. The group of young men still lounged under the tree but she became aware that one of them had lazily risen to follow her across the empty compound toward the public market. Nearing the exit she laid her bike on the ground and turned to face him.

He smiled charmingly and pointed to her purse. "I like purse," he said, extending his hand.

"I like it, too," she said.

"You give purse, please."

"No," she said, and adjusted her weight to an on-guard stance, feet apart, one foot pointing to one side, the other forward, and weight distributed equally between them. When he made his lunge forward she was ready for him and with the edge of her hand she karate-slashed him across the jaw. He reeled backward, stunned. She picked up her bicycle and as she resumed her exit from the compound she discovered a blond-haired young man staring at her in astonishment.

"I say, I saw through the opening what was going to happen," he said, making way for her and her bicycle in the passageway. "I saw you both. I was going to rescue you."

"That's very kind of you," she said, "and I'm sorry I denied you the pleasure."

He grinned. "You're damn good at karate, I'll say that. Black belt?"

She shook her head. "Brown belt."

He grinned. "You must be the Mrs. Pollifax who flew in yesterday, news travels fast here. I'm World Aid—the experimental farm. Tony Dahl."

They shook hands. "But what were you doing back *there*?" he asked.

"I made the wrong turn and got lost," she told him.

"Well—now you know," he said. "Going back to the palace?"

When she nodded he said, "Yes, you'd better, or you might be followed, still. I'm here for some peanuts and a pair of scissors. . . . Come see the experimental farm!"

"I will," she promised. "Happy shopping."

Mounting her bicycle she pedaled furiously back to the palace.

There was no time to see Kadi alone on her return because when they finally met again it was to tour the second palace with Sammat that was now called Government House. Sammat seemed determined and pleased about showing it to them personally, and Mrs. Pollifax could understand his need: a need to remind himself—and to show them—what he had accomplished before vicious rumors began to tarnish his accomplishments. Above all, she thought, he drew comfort from Kadi, whom he had known since childhood, and so the Makarov pistol remained in her purse. They set off on foot for the nearby palace, built by the late President-for-Life Chinyata during the years he had spent looting the nation's treasury.

"It's not nearly so grand as the palace we've just left," explained Sammat. "It was the first one built. When Simoko came to power heaven only knows why he had to compete with a dead man, the very man he'd assassinated—ego, immortality, who knows? In any case he spent twice the money on *his* palace."

This was obvious: the older building was built of sun-dried clay, painted white; its rooms were smaller, less pretentious, and there was no glittering marble entrance hall. It did, however, have a splendid auditorium, although unfortunately the Picadilly Popcorn Rock Band was not rehearsing this afternoon, a disappointment to Kadi. It housed the radio station, which broadcast from 3 P.M. to 8 P.M., the offices of the *Ubangiba Free Press*, and of World Aid, and it was headquarters for the lottery.

"Lottery?" echoed Kadi.

Sammat nodded. "It's quite a success. Tickets cost only a few *pince*, the drawing's held every thirty days, and the prize is one hundred fifty *gwar*. It gives people hope. It will also," he added, "help pay for the power station we'll need once the coal mine is operative."

The tour was only moderately interesting to Mrs.

Pollifax until they reached the basement where the newspaper office and the presses had been installed. Sammat said, "The presses should be rolling now, the weekly paper's due out in the morning." He called into the pressroom, "What's wrong, Mbuza?"

A cheerful black man in a white coverall shouted back, "Small repair, *mfumo*, they be good workers." Sammat strolled inside, followed by Kadi, but Mrs. Pollifax chose to wander down the hall and peer into the empty newsroom. It was occupied by two desks, three old manual typewriters, a copy machine, file cabinets, and a long shelf full of papers, but a copy of the *Ubangiba Free Press* lay on the editor's desk. Dated a week ago, she glanced at it with interest. Under a page-one banner headline: MR. MWANGO AND WORLD AID PREDICT GOOD HARVEST, there was a smaller one: INTERVIEW WITH MR. DICKSON ZIMBA, SOTO REPRESENTATIVE TO COMMITTEE FOR A CONSTITUTION.

The interview occupied half a page.

Running her eyes down the story, Mrs. Pollifax was caught up by a particularly provocative question asked by the interviewer, one Johnson Sovi.

Sovi: We have a new and young head of state, Mr. Zimba, soon to be our king. In the months that he has been at Government

House, how would you summarize his performance?

Mr. Zimba: I'm impressed by his energy but, frankly, not by his goals for Ubangiba. To me he's a white man with a black skin. He's enjoyed all the advantages that the British colonials gave to his grandfather, King Zammat, he attended a mission school run by a white man, he has spent the past four years in America, and see how he brings in white men and women to organize us. It's back to colonialist days.

Startled, she read on:

Sovi: And in what direction, Mr. Zimba, would you prefer that he steer the country?

Mr. Zimba: Not to this "Food First," back-to-the-land movement. Ridiculous! He speaks of bringing the country into the twentieth century, yet refuses factories and investment. He's obsessed with cooperatives and fertilizer, as if that is the only way to increase employment. He speaks of going forward and takes us backward.

Hearing Kadi's and Sammy's footsteps, Mrs. Pollifax quickly replaced the newspaper on the desk.

Sammat looked amused. "Oh, there's no need to hide it, that's last week's issue and I've read it. The next one comes out tomorrow."

"If I finish reading this one," inquired Mrs. Pollifax, "will I learn what Dickson Zimba wants for your country?"

"I don't think he has the slightest idea," Sammat said, "and I hope I'm not sounding condescending when I say that. He's hostile to World Aid, but says he wants factories, which would mean European investment and even *more* non-Africans overrunning the country, and we simply don't have the infrastructure for high commerce yet." He shook his head. "Our top priority has to be growing our own food, which we did very well before Chinyata and Simoko. Build just one factory here in Languka, and seven out of ten farmers would abandon their farms and head to the city for a job they've no skills for; shantytown would triple in size, we'd have to import food again, and we'd go broke."

Mrs. Pollifax smiled. "Well said! But I don't think he likes you, Sammat."

"Oh, that scarcely matters," Sammat said dismissingly.

But Mrs. Pollifax wondered if it might not matter. She decided that she would like very much to meet this Mr. Zimba and judge for herself if he was a danger to which Sammat was blind. Too *much* ambition, she thought, could lead to ruthlessness.

They strolled back to Simoko's palace, a short walk along a street with an outdoor market and offices that had sprung up to serve the palaces: the courthouse, a small post office, several houses of business with signs in their windows: NATIONAL MILLING COMPANY; JONES ENTERPRISES LTD.; LANGUKA TRADING STORE; FARMERS CO-OP OF UBANGIBA. The sound of a siren could be heard in the distance but it was only another city sound until it grew louder and closer.

"Police?" said Kadi.

"Sounds more like an ambulance," Sammat told her.

As they reached the palace entrance a renovated Land Rover, painted white and bearing a huge red cross, raced down the drive, stopped, two men jumped out, unfolded a stretcher and began fumbling with something or someone in the rear.

"What is it?" asked Sammat, calling to them.

One of the men turned a panicky face to him. "*Yanga mfumo*, another lion attack. *Mkambo*! He be still with breath, but—" He shook his head. Together he and his man lifted a bloody body from the car and placed it on the stretcher. A nurse rushed out, followed by Dr. Merrick and the native M.D., Dr. Kasonde.

A sheet had been thrown over the man in the Land Rover, but it fell to one side as he was placed on the stretcher, and Mrs. Pollifax caught her breath at what she saw: a torn throat, a dozen claw marks across his face and shoulders. She turned away, shocked and nauseated. *Poor man, poor man,* she whispered over and over. He was carried quickly through the doors, Dr. Merrick at his side.

Death number four, she realized bleakly.

Sammat followed the stretcher into the emergency room and Mrs. Pollifax nearly wept at the stern and sickened look on his face.

5

Later that afternoon Mrs. Pollifax left her room and began the process of descending the two long staircases for dinner in the hospital's staff cafeteria. Reaching the balcony she glanced down into the huge entrance hall, usually filled with patients waiting to be called into the emergency room; the benches were empty now except for one on which Dr. Merrick sat, leaning wearily against the wall. Finishing her descent she walked across the marble floor and joined him. "Will the man live?" she asked.

"Still hanging on—barely," he said in a depressed voice.

"Are you resting or waiting for someone?"

"The police inspector's due any minute, I don't want my patients to see him, it'll only upset them. You saw the latest casualty, then?"

She nodded. "I saw." Frowning, she said, "Tell me, is there any pattern to these killings? I mean, do the victims appear to be selected at random, or do they have something in common?"

Dr. Merrick sighed. "You speak of one killer but I'm not sure there's only one," he said. "Since Dr. Kasonde and I share the responsibility of being both coroner and forensic department we've mentioned to the police a certain dissimilarity in the wounds of one of the four victims. The first one, actually, which could mean anything."

"Like what?"

"Well, the lacerations on the three men killed here in the capital suggest a sharper instrument, they match in depth and length. The farmer in the south—the first death—had shallower claw marks on throat and body. No less fatal—it found the jugular vein—but shallower. Jonas and the snack bar man, Silumo Makada, had much deeper lacerations, and so did poor Tiamoko Barau this afternoon.

"As to your question," he added, "they *so far* appear to be random killings."

"So far?"

He said wearily, "You don't think it's going to stop, do you, until the murderer is found?"

"But the motive?"

He said dryly, "I think you know that as well as I do. One need only observe people's reactions to assume that, so far, the motive behind all this is to terrify."

"Does it terrify *you*?" she asked.

He smiled derisively. "Let's just say that I don't plan to go out alone after dark, or find myself the only pedestrian in a back alley in daylight, and I strongly suggest that you and young Kadi do your walking on the palace grounds. In the garden . . . Ah, here's my policeman—a good one, by the way. Chief Inspector Banda," he said, rising to greet a brisk, slender man in his thirties wearing an immaculate dark-green uniform. He was clean-shaven, with a thick knot of frown lines between his eyes, but he appeared to have carefully removed all expression from his face. Wasting no time in pleasantries he nodded to Mrs. Pollifax and said, "Shall we talk now?" The two men walked away in the direction of the gardens. Mrs. Pollifax rose and continued on her way to the cafeteria to meet Kadi.

Ice cream had been promised for dessert that night but the freezer had broken down—"again," said Rakia, Kadi's friend, the nurse. "Pretty grand, having ice cream," she added with a broad smile. "The cafeteria's only for the hospital staff, because they're not natives and used to different food, but they let me take some of it home to my children. But who can carry ice cream? No loss to me, but I'm sorry for you, Mrs. Pollifax."

Mrs. Pollifax smiled at her. "It's very drinkable and just as good melted."

A plain woman, Rakia, but a cheerful one. A figured red headscarf framed her round-cheeked, pockmarked black face with its full lips and bright eyes. A loyal friend, too, remembered Mrs. Pollifax, since it was she who had helped smuggle Kadi out of the country after her parents' death, and she fervently hoped that Rakia's seven children had a good father.

"Well—I've got to go," Rakia said, wrapping leftover chicken in a paper towel and stowing it in her bag.

"Ride your bicycle fast," Mrs. Pollifax heard herself say, recalling Dr. Merrick's warnings, and Rakia gave her a quick, sharp glance.

"Yes," she said, "you've heard, then." And with a glance at her watch, "Almost dark, I'm late. 'Night, Kadi." She gave her a hug and walked out of the room, sturdy and broad-hipped, changed now out of uniform into a blue shirt and black skirt which Mrs. Pollifax thought very sensible, and much less conspicuous in the dark than a white uniform, *and now I'm allowing these deaths to affect me, too,* she realized, and said to Kadi, "Let's finish our melted ice cream in the garden, I've something important to give you."

"A *present?*"

"Not your typical gift," Mrs. Pollifax told her, "but a useful one."

They walked down the hall toward the hospital kitchen and carried their bowls and spoons out of the service entrance into the garden. The sun had set, and darkness had fallen with the abruptness of a curtain. Lights from the kitchen spilled circles of light across the ground, turning the wall of bougainvillea a garish pink and illuminating one side of the canvas tent in which they'd had dinner the previous evening. Beyond it rose the dark shapes of new tents, and Mrs. Pollifax remembered these were being erected for the coronation, and that Sammat despaired of their cost. "Fifty elegant tents!" he'd said. "They could feed a dozen families for two weeks. It's ridiculous!"

Kadi and Mrs. Pollifax pulled canvas chairs up to a table near the windows and sat down. "Definitely cooler out here," Kadi said, "and isn't Rakia a lovely person? The women in this country are so—so *strong*."

"Lovely," agreed Mrs. Pollifax, delighting in the coolness on her arms and face after the heat of the day. The air was fragrant with the scent of flowers, the sound of crickets made a companionable backdrop and muffled voices could be heard from the kitchen. Mrs. Pollifax began fumbling in her purse for the Makarov 9mm to present to Kadi when, abruptly, the peacefulness of the night was violated by the sound of a loud hammering in the garden.

"Tent pegs?" Kadi wondered, frowning.

"They're certainly pounding relentlessly," contributed Mrs. Pollifax. "This present isn't gift-wrapped," she began, but Kadi interrupted.

"Who could be working so late?" asked Kadi. "That's an awful sound, they'll wake the patients in surgery, don't they realize that?"

"Kadi—" began Mrs. Pollifax, but Kadi had already slipped out of her chair. "Kadi, no!" she cried. "Kadi, don't—come back, you shouldn't—"

But Kadi had vanished beyond the circle of light and into the darkness.

Mrs. Pollifax had half risen from her chair to follow her when she heard a sound of scuffling and then a scream. At once she was on her feet and running as she called out, "Kadi? Kadi, I'm coming!" Stumbling over tent pegs and pushing aside shrubbery she would later wonder if it was the sound of her voice that saved Kadi, as over and over she called her name in the darkness until, "H-here," said a faint voice, and Kadi burst into tears. "He—he—"

"We need light—badly," cried Mrs. Pollifax, but Kadi's scream had been heard and it was Dr. Merrick who came rushing out with a flashlight.

"Who's there?" he shouted. "Who screamed?"

"Over here," said Mrs. Pollifax, "Kadi's been

hurt." When his flashlight moved in the wrong direction she called again, "Here—over *here*!"

His light found them, to illuminate Kadi curled up on the ground and rocking back and forth, one hand gripping her left arm. "It hurts," she sobbed.

The two of them knelt beside her. "Hold the flashlight," said Dr. Merrick, handing it to Mrs. Pollifax, and he gently pried Kadi's hand away from her arm.

With the arm exposed to the light, Mrs. Pollifax shuddered at the scarlet gash running the length of the arm, the skin neatly sliced open, leaving a long red line, not bleeding yet, except for a bubble of blood near Kadi's elbow. "Who was it, Kadi?" she asked.

"I don't know, I don't know," cried Kadi. "He came out of the dark—just a shape—and he had a knife. And I fought him, I fought him, but he was so—so *strong*," she said on a sob.

Dr. Merrick said, "I hope it was just a knife. Kadi, I'm going to carry you into the infirmary now, let your arm hang loose. I won't hurt you but we've got to treat this at once, you hear?"

But Kadi had fainted—"shock," said Dr. Merrick—and it was an unconscious Kadi who was carried out of the garden, down the hall, and through the empty marble lobby into the emergency room.

Mrs. Pollifax turned and looked back into the

garden before she followed: it was dark and silent now, and she wondered: had it been a thief bent on robbing the palace whom Kadi had disturbed by accident? Had the hammering been started deliberately to entice *someone* into the garden, or had it been specifically Kadi whom the person in the garden wanted to harm?

She was remembering what Moses had said: *When there have been three deaths there is no pity.*

As had been said over and over, news traveled swiftly in Languka. Sammat, meeting with tribal elders in the old palace, left them to rush to the emergency room only half an hour after Kadi's attack, and once assured that she was in good hands he rushed away again. At seven the next morning Joseph brought a bag of sunflower seeds for Kadi; at half past seven Rakia arrived with lovingness and a cheerful smile; and one by one strangers came with gifts: a knot of tiny wildflowers gleaned from a shady place, a carved whistle, a few eggs, live chickens.

Rakia said to a marveling Mrs. Pollifax, "They not *all* know Kadi, they bring gifts because she is daughter to Dr. and Mrs. Hopkirk, they were very loved. We feel our *amakolo* with us always, you know."

"*Amakolo?*" repeated Mrs. Pollifax.

Kadi said drowsily from her bed, "Ancestors."

"An-*cestors*," Rakia agreed, nodding vigorously. "We make shrines and sacrifices to them. Kadi has good *amakolo*, see how lucky she was!"

At noon Dr. Merrick brought in the freshly printed *Ubangiba Free Press.* "Front page, Kadi!" he said. "Mrs. Pollifax, read it to her."

And it was true: near the top of page one, sandwiched between a report on the co-op farms and plans for the coronation, there had been inserted a small headline: HOPKIRK DAUGHTER ATTACKED. The report read, "Last night, in the palace garden, Miss Kadi Hopkirk, daughter of the late Dr. and Mrs. Hopkirk, was attacked with a knife by an unknown person or persons. She had been seated with a friend drinking in the coolness of the evening"— "poetic touch," murmured Mrs. Pollifax—"when Miss Hopkirk heard noises in the garden and left her friend to investigate. Moments later she screamed, and was discovered felled by her assailant, with a knife slash the length of her arm. 'Definitely a knife,' emphasized Chief Inspector Banda. Miss Hopkirk is now recovering in our hospital's infirmary. She is here for the coronation of King Zammat's grandson, Sammat, at his personal invitation."

"Note the quote from Inspector Banda, 'Definitely a knife,' " pointed out Dr. Merrick.

"But it *was* a knife, wasn't it?"

"Oh yes—if people will *believe* that."

Sammat, joining them, said, "And now I must increase the palace guards and station several in the palace garden—too late, of course! Mrs. Pollifax, I'm about to visit the old royal compound where the kings lived, and with Kadi out of circulation today I wonder if you'd care to see it."

He *was* nice, thought Mrs. Pollifax. Thoughtful, too, since she was feeling quite useless, sitting with a well-attended Kadi. "Gladly," she said, "I'd like that very much."

"Yes, do go," Kadi told her. "When you get back I shall be up, I promise you. I don't want to miss tomorrow's ride south to see the backhoe celebration!"

"Only if Dr. Kasonde or Dr. Merrick say so," warned Mrs. Pollifax.

As Sammat led her through the crowded entrance hall and outside to a dusty Land Rover he murmured, "Nasty business, this."

Mrs. Pollifax agreed. "Do you think her attacker was someone bent on robbery, or could it have been—" But she found that she couldn't put words to her fears.

"Inspector Banda's found a footprint—a clue," he told her reassuringly, and with a smile, "Just like one of your American detective novels, a clue."

She said no more; obviously it had not yet occurred to him that it might not have been a random attack on Kadi. To tell him what worried her would only add more to his considerable burdens.

"You won't be away from Kadi long," he said, not understanding her concern. "The compound's not far, there's only a path to it now, which makes for a bumpy ride. . . . Actually, I wish the coronation could be held there," he said wistfully, "but of course the sacred gold stool—you saw that in April—and the royal drums, the scepter and tapestries and robes were long ago moved to President Chinyata's palace, and then to Simoko's palace. I'll show them to you another day, perhaps."

Just beyond the shantytown Sammat swerved off to the right and followed an ill-defined path. They lurched and bounced over untilled earth until up ahead Mrs. Pollifax saw the ruins of a wall, surrounded by acacia trees.

Sammat, stopping the Land Rover, said simply, "Here in this place lives the soul of our people. From wherever we came—and our legends speak of a migration from the west centuries ago—this is where the first shrine was made to our ancestors, and where generations of kings lived and ruled."

Startled, she said, "Your grandfather, too?"

"Yes and no," he said, smiling. "This was still the royal palace when he was born, and yes, he was born here but grew up in Languka." He added proudly, "He was a very learned man, the first king to be educated abroad. It was he who negotiated with the British, you know. For our independence."

As he helped her down from the Land Rover, he added, without expression, "The later royal compound—my home—I can't show you. President Chinyata ordered it destroyed when he took over the country—records, books, everything precious and old. 'We begin a new era,' he announced to the people as he watched the buildings burn."

"What a terrible thing to do," said Mrs. Pollifax.

"Yes. He not only destroyed much of our history but also a home that I loved."

He led her through the ruins of what had once been an entrance gate, and they emerged into a great open space, much of it overgrown with grass. Sammat, pointing, said, "Over there—see?—that was once the ceremonial hall." She turned and saw the skeletal bones of a long arched hall, open at either end, its sheathing worn away by wind and sun and time. Scattered around the great circle were roofless shells of what had been huts. "Offices," Sammat explained. "Offices for the war chief, the administrative head, the controller of finances, the interpreter of oracles, and the chief judge.

"And here is the shrine," Sammat said, pausing next to a well-kept line of attached conical huts, the roofs freshly thatched. "I won't be long," he told her. "Feel free to walk around, but watch out for scorpions."

A private matter, then: she was not to see the shrine.

As he vanished into the shadowed entrance a faint breeze stirred the grass and made silky, whispering sounds. A place of many ghosts, she thought, and she remembered what Carstairs had told her of the country's history, how it had first been heard of in the eighteenth century, when a lone survivor of a Tuareg raid in the Sahara had been rescued by a tribe called the Shambi and taken to "a pastoral land where the Soto and the Shambi lived in peace."

Perhaps it was to this same royal compound that he'd been brought over two centuries ago.

The local myth, Carstairs had told her dryly, was that, centuries before then, a quarrel had arisen between Chief Mobolu of the Soto tribe, and Zammat, chief of the Shambi, and to avoid war the two chiefs were bound together in the throne room, and a pair of poisonous snakes released, so that the gods might speak and choose which man was to survive and to rule. The unfortunate Mobolu had died—and it was Zammat whom the gods had favored—and from this had come the pair of inter-twined serpents portrayed on the Ubangiban flag, and engraved on the sacred royal gold ring.

The rest of its history was more pedestrian: the country had been unwillingly inherited by the Brit-ish at the Treaty of Versailles but in the ensuing

years their attempts to make its economy profitable
had failed: it was a landlocked country, it was
small, and its only exports were animal hides,
sunflower seeds, and ground nuts. England, she
thought, must have felt somewhat relieved to grant
the country its independence.

The sun was hot, and Sammat's warning about
scorpions inhibited exploration. Wandering outside
the gate she found a rock on which to sit and to
consider feelings that she could neither define nor
name. She could admit to ghosts of the past, but
there was more to her reaction than this. Perhaps
she was experiencing what Sammat had called the
soul of his country, but also of Africa itself, where
Time had begun, and Man as well. Here in the
ruins of this old palace no sounds intruded, the
leaves in the grove of trees hung limp and still,
there was only the earth: earthen compound, roofs
of thatch that had grown out of the earth, walls of
clay, dung, and thatch, posts and walls carved lov-
ingly out of wood.

She thought how close to the earth the people
had lived, and that if there were such entities as
Earth Spirits it would be here they lived, not in the
new palaces of glass and marble, metal and plastic.
Sammat trusted the earth, he wanted Ubangiban
farms to prosper, grow fertile and feed all the people, as it had fed them before dictators had raped
the villages and countryside. If Sammat was driven

out by these terrible rumors of sorcery what would happen to this sun-baked country of bush and greening fields and desert, to the hospital, the free press, and the new crop experiments?

The appearance of a guinea fowl interrupted her thoughts and she smiled as she watched it rush indignantly out of the grove of trees to vanish behind the walls of the compound. Yet with the flight of the guinea fowl something had changed, and suddenly Mrs. Pollifax felt uneasy.

I am being watched, she thought in dismay, *I can feel it, there is someone hiding in among those trees, it's why the guinea fowl rushed out of the grove.*

She stood up, uncertain what to do. Her first impulse was at once to walk into the copse of trees and learn who was there, but remembering the attack on Kadi, remembering the lion deaths she hesitated and then Sammat walked out of the shrine room and the gate and said, "Shall we go now?"

She did not mention the sensation of having been watched. Instead, as they drove away she said politely, "Is it true that in Africa you *worship* your ancestors?"

Sammat laughed. "You know, at Yale I took a course in comparative religions, and Catholicism interested me very much, with its many saints. I learned that Catholics pray to their saints—all of whom are dead—and light candles to them, offer gifts, and ask for help and guidance. Just so do we revere our ancestors. We pray to them, hold festivals for them, and offer sacrifices—like gifts—and hope for guidance and help. Is there so great a difference? I don't know. We like to believe our ancestors still watch over us, even," he added, smiling, "if not many of them were saintlike."

Curious, she asked, "And did you make a sacrifice at the shrine?"

He said soberly, "Of course . . . and prayed with all my heart for help just now."

She nodded. There was no need for him to explain why.

6

At five o'clock the next morning a knock at the door woke Mrs. Pollifax, and she stumbled out of bed, half-asleep, to find Joseph in the hall with a tray of breakfast food in his hands. *"Moni!"* he said, "it be five o'clock."

Mrs. Pollifax realized that one must not feel annoyed with a man who had saved their lives on that first brief visit to Ubangiba, but for a moment she found his knock unforgivable, because she wanted more sleep and Joseph looked incredibly awake and even cheerful. *Definitely a morning person,* she thought crossly, and noticing the gun in his holster she remembered that she still carried the Makarov in her purse. While she ate her hard-boiled egg and porridge she wondered what to do with it for this day, and having been warned of pickpockets she finally stuffed it deep inside of Kadi's knapsack.

A surprise awaited her downstairs. Dr. Merrick

had given in to Kadi's pleas to see the backhoe celebration in the south, but *only* if she remained in
the bus and watched the occasion from the window.
Mrs. Pollifax made no protest, since Dr. Merrick
would be going, too; it was his day off and he'd
volunteered to drive one of the buses, leaving surgery to Dr. Kasonde; they would ride with him.
Walking out of the palace forty-five minutes later,
and seeing the three buses waiting for them, she
exclaimed, "Well!" and smiled.

Kadi, emerging from the infirmary with her
arm heavily swathed in bandages, joined her and
said, "Wow!"

The first bus was a riot of yellow sunflowers
painted on a background of bright red, the second
bus was a hot pink, with dizzyingly blue polka
dots, and the third was black, with colorful drawings of children playing, men at work, and women
with baskets on their heads, all of them walking in
a procession around the bus carriage. A loud-
speaker was blaring music for the crowd surround-
ing the buses, and the men were equally as colorful
in printed cotton robes, all of them chattering and
shouting to add to the cacophony. The chiefs and
sub-chiefs had arrived; the only white face to be
seen among them was that of Dr. Merrick, looking
much younger in jeans and a denim shirt.

"Hop in," he said with a wink at Kadi, and as
the passengers filed into the bus their names were

hurled at Mrs. Pollifax and Kadi. "Chief Kampemba," said Dr. Merrick. "Judge Mutale of the Ubangiban court . . . Chief Chibabila . . . Mr. Ernest Malima of the Agricultural School . . . Mr. Kamuzo Chibambo of the Textile School . . ." Each courteously leaned down to smile at Kadi in her seat, and to speak of their *chisoni*—their sorrow—at her being hurt.

"And Mr. Dickson Zimba . . ."

On hearing his name Mrs. Pollifax looked up sharply. No one had mentioned his being so prim-looking a man, with such a disapproving glare. He was thin and wiry—*like a coiled spring,* thought Mrs. Pollifax—and wore gold-rimmed spectacles that magnified intense black eyes. He was the only man not in native garb; he wore a thin black suit and a white shirt. *To set himself apart,* guessed Mrs. Pollifax, and she nodded to him politely. He took the seat behind them, occupying it exclusively.

They left as the sun rose, a huge and perfect circle of brilliant orange that scattered the shadows and slowly devoured the predawn dusk. As it rose higher it brought with it intimations of the warmth that by noon would burgeon into relentless heat.

In the seat behind her Dickson Zimba leaned forward to say importantly, "I am Dickson Zimba, and you—Mrs. Poltiflack?—you are shocked by the poverty of our poor country?"

Turning to look at him she felt attacked by those piercing black eyes. She said sturdily, "Not so poor that good leadership can't bring great change—and it's Pollifax, not Poltiflack."

"*Hah!*" he said and leaned back, saying no more.

She too sat back, interested in seeing the country outside of Languka, and since it was a drive of over two hours she was to see a great deal of it: groves of acacia trees followed by long, flat, dull stretches of bush and scrub, a school, a field of men tying up great bundles of wooden sticks—"not wood," said Kadi, "those are millet spikes drying in the sun." A dusty truck occasionally passed them, as well as the thrice-daily bus to Languka. Women walked along the road with babies in slings across their backs, and now and then a woman sat behind a modest roadside stall, selling vegetables, bread, and bottles of soda.

Kadi soon fell asleep. Across the aisle two chiefs were conversing in clipped English about what the discovery of coal could do for their country, and Mrs. Pollifax frankly eavesdropped. Was it best, they argued, to provide electricity for the villages? Artesian wells were vital, of course, but how many, and could they be evenly distributed between desert and the farmland that most urgently needed water, without the Soto tribe objecting and harassing the government for an equal share?

Dickson Zimba entered this argument and assured them that yes, the Soto tribe would object and would sue if necessary, now that Ubangiba had a high court.

Rather maliciously one of the chiefs pointed out that Ubangiba had no constitution yet, thanks to certain people who disrupted discussions and quarreled over every word. At this point Dr. Merrick halted the bus beside the road, opened a Styrofoam container, and distributed lukewarm orange soda, tea, and bottles of *mtibi*, the native sweet beer. Kadi, waking from her nap, said, "Oh good, my throat feels like sandpaper. We must be almost there." She laughed. "Rakia says the foreman brought from England to oversee the mine is a Cockney. Like Michael Caine," she added knowingly, and when Mrs. Pollifax gave her an amused glance she grinned and said, "You have to remember I saw my first movie at fifteen, I've had to make up for lost time. The first film I saw was on television, *The Ipcress File*; I *loved* the way Michael Caine broke eggs for an omelette."

"Broke eggs?"

Kadi nodded. "*Tenderly.* I'd never seen a man cook before."

Following their rest stop Dr. Merrick drove on again under a whitening sky toward the long line of hills that loomed now on the horizon, but Mrs. Pollifax could stay awake no longer; she closed her eyes and slept. When the bus came to a stop she woke up and saw they had arrived, and that the hills had turned into mountains now that they were under them and in their long shadow.

A base camp had been set up here for the miners, furnished with half a dozen tents, and *I do hope there won't be speeches,* thought Mrs. Pollifax. The backhoe gleamed bright and yellow in the sun and was surrounded by people, in fact it looked as if every neighboring village had been emptied to view this historic event.

As Mrs. Pollifax looked at the scene more closely, however, she thought the crowd did not seem to be behaving as crowds should: there appeared to be rather a lot of arm waving, and when Dr. Merrick swung open the bus door Mrs. Pollifax heard shouting and then a woman screaming.

Seeing the buses arrive, a swarm of boys raced toward them, shouting, *"Imfa! Imfa! Imfa!"*

Dr. Merrick said clearly, "What the hell!" and leapt out of the bus.

Mrs. Pollifax exclaimed more modestly, "What on earth—!" and bolted after him.

When the children saw Sammat disembarking from the third bus they swerved toward him; what Sammat said was unheard but abruptly, like lemmings, the boys all changed direction and headed back to the camp again, but Dr. Merrick and Mrs. Pollifax had reached the site first. The problem was seen at once: in order to entertain the huge audience that had been waiting since dawn, the foreman, Callahan, had started up his machine and had made a preliminary opening at the base of the hill to demonstrate what a backhoe could do. What had been uncovered was a skull, still half-embedded in the earth, its eyeless sockets staring back at a shocked foreman and a shocked and frightened crowd.

Dr. Merrick knelt beside the skull and examined it. A minute later he stood and called out, "Steady, everyone! *Not* a new death. Not *mkambo!*" When no one listened he shouted, "Hey! *Not mkambo . . . manda!*" and desperately, "Damn it, what's the word . . . *Manda! Kalamba! Kale kale, kale kale.*"

"What does all that mean?" asked Mrs. Pollifax.

He grinned. "I *hope* I'm telling them that it's an old grave, very old. I know *kale kale* means 'long ago,' because all their legends begin with 'long long ago' but that's the only word I can be sure of."

They had heard him: the hysteria was fading. Dr. Merrick told Sammat hurriedly, "This skull is old, really old, possibly a hundred years old or more, and friable. You've got to cover this skull right away or it'll turn to dust, it's the peat that's preserved it. You just may have stumbled on an ancient tomb here, Sammat."

Dickson Zimba said impatiently, "But we want *coal*."

Sammat turned to the foreman. "Is this precisely where the geologists recommended you start? They found no skull."

The foreman pointed west. "Farther along, guv—by the red flags—but you can see we're nearer the road and the wells 'ere. It's 'andier, the men'll be thirsty in this 'eat. 'Ot as 'ell it'll be soon. What I thought was, if there's coal *there*, there's coal 'ere."

"Yes, but you must at once move the backhoe farther west now," Sammat pointed out. "You see what's here."

The foreman glanced suspiciously past Sammat. "Them witch doctors aren't with you, are they? Spent the 'ole day here yesterday! Creepy chaps."

"Not here," Sammat assured him, and Callahan returned to the backhoe, climbed aboard it and prepared to move.

Mrs. Pollifax said, "But this is exciting, Sammat, it could be an ancestor of yours!"

"I feel only cross now," he told her crossly. "This is not good, it frightens the villagers. Someone with a shovel—you," he said, pointing to a boy. "Help Dr. Merrick bury the skull, will you?"

"Carefully—carefully," warned Dr. Merrick.

"Let me help," said Mrs. Pollifax. The backhoe had roared to life, and like a pied piper was leading everyone westward to the new site. She was sure now there would be speeches, probably long ones, and she thought a very old skull much less depressing.

The boy waited, shovel in hand, bright-eyed and interested as the three of them looked over the situation. He said his name was Reuben, and where was he to dig?

"It mustn't be touched," Dr. Merrick said, scowling. "I think we just cover it lightly with the earth removed by the backhoe. You speak English, Reuben?"

"I speak much *good* English," the boy said. "You wish me to carry earth there to here. . . . You think it ancestor tomb, sir? If thus, there should be sacrifice made, and prayers."

"No time for sacrifices, *you* say a prayer but cover the skull first."

Mrs. Pollifax said dryly, "They all seem to know of the lion deaths, even here."

"A pity, yes."

Reuben was about to lift his first shovelful of earth when Mrs. Pollifax said, "Wait a minute." She had noticed something in the far corner of the hole, quite separate from the skull. Kneeling, she peered inside, reached in and gently pried loose a small object foreign to the earth. Brushing the soil from it she said ruefully, "I shouldn't have done this, should I, but—*kale kale*, Dr. Merrick?"

The three of them, Reuben as well, bent over her discovery. What she held in the palm of her hand was a circle of metal—iron or bronze—a little over two inches in diameter, with an openwork center laced with a curious, raised design. There were two metal loops at one edge, suggesting that once it must have been linked to a chain.

"Snakes," said Reuben, leaning close to look, and pointing with one long dark finger.

Dr. Merrick nodded. "You're right, those serpentine lines are worn, but they're definitely snakes. Very decorative! A well-cast piece, old, and obviously in the earth a long time."

"Would it belong with the skull, perhaps?"

"Perhaps." Touching it, Dr. Merrick said thoughtfully, "I think we show this to Tony Dahl, the World Aid chap at the farm. He spent each of his college summers with an archaeological team in Egypt, he can tell us if we've stumbled across what I think we have. He's at the Experimental Crop Farm, we'll take this to him after lunch, you'll like him."

"I've met him," said Mrs. Pollifax, and with a twinkle added, "At the black market."

Merrick gave her a sharp glance. "You really went there?"

"Yes, and just what *are* you thinking?" she asked, wanting to hear him say it.

"I'm thinking that our friend, the future King Zammat IX, may have an archaeological find on his hands here that *could* be of far more value—historically at least—than his coal mine. This is really old, maybe Bronze Age, but Tony can tell us. . . . A pity he wasn't here to see the skull but this should be enough to intrigue him. The only problem," added Dr. Merrick with a frown, "is how superstitious the natives are going to be about this, coupled with rumors of sorcery and four lion murders. . . ."

If there were speeches scheduled at the mine's official opening they had been brief, to avoid the midday heat, and by the middle of the morning they were on their way back to the capital, leaving the backhoe to its excavating, with a crew of young Ubangibans prepared to shore up the entrance and wield shovels and pickaxes. Each visitor from the capital returned with a souvenir: a small piece of hard black rock, brittle and bright, and undeniably a sample of anthracite coal. Mrs. Pollifax noticed however that no one mentioned the skull that had been inadvertently unearthed. Once at the palace the guests poured out of their buses, smiling, forming groups to talk, and Kadi, holding Mrs. Pollifax's arm and walking slowly, made her way to Sammat to congratulate him.

He turned at once to her. "Did the trip tire you? Are you all right?"

"I'm okay. I missed most of the fun but I was glad to be up and out again."

With a glance at her heavily wrapped arm he grinned. "Just like a mummy!" His eyes moved beyond her and he frowned. "Now what on earth is wrong with Joseph?"

They turned to see Joseph pushing his way ruthlessly through the crowd, shoving several people heedlessly out of the way. The usually calm and efficient Joseph looked frantic, his eyes blazing with anger. Trapped for the moment behind two men he shouted over their heads, "*Mfumo*, a terrible thing. Thievery! Burglary!"

Sammat regarded Joseph with astonishment. "What's happened?"

Joseph broke through the crowd to reach them at last. "While you gone—thievery!" he repeated.

"*Heya*, what can have been stolen to excite you so, Joseph?" asked Sammat. "You know Simoko's gold is stored in London and our funds in the bank here."

"No no, *records*," gasped Joseph. "The secret files kept by President Simoko. In the strong room. Nbuzu Simakonda reported to me just ten minutes ago! He find door not locked!"

Sammat said sharply, "Show me." And to Mrs. Pollifax and Kadi, "This really *is* a serious business, you must excuse me!"

"We'll come with you," said Mrs. Pollifax, with what she admitted was outrageous cheek, but since neither Sammat nor Joseph remonstrated she and Kadi followed in their wake, rushing behind them as they made their way through the entrance hall, past the emergency room, and turned to the right at the door to the hospital kitchen. Leaving kitchen sounds behind them they continued past a long row of doors and stopped at the last one, where the door was ajar.

Down five cement steps they descended into what appeared to Mrs. Pollifax to be a cement bunker lighted by two feeble lightbulbs. In the middle of the room stood a young man in a palace guard's uniform with three stripes on his sleeve. Behind him rose a ceiling-high latticework gate of iron, with a padlock, that guarded a smaller room—a vault—fitted with ceiling-high metal drawers. Several of the drawers had been strewn across the floor; the dim overhead light showed dark cavities in the row upon row of them, disturbing their awesome metal symmetry.

"Sergeant Simakonda," said the guard, saluting. "*Mfumo*, I see this and run to tell."

"A good thing you did," Sammat said absently, walking up to the iron gate. "Why is it locked now?"

"I no touch," said the sergeant, backing away.

Joseph said in horror, "You mean the lock wasn't broken?"

"No, sir."

"Picked," said Mrs. Pollifax knowledgeably, following Sammat and looking at it.

" 'Picked?' " Joseph echoed.

"If it wasn't attacked with a sledgehammer it has to have been picked." Remembering all that she'd learned from John Sebastian Farrell and Robin Bourke-Jones, she explained, "It's a word thieves use. To pick a lock like this would need a little time and a special tool, but a professional could probably do it in ten minutes. It happened during the night? What was kept here?"

Eyes narrowed, Sammat said softly, "We've not had the time to go through Simoko's files, there's been so much to do. We've been naive, Joseph—*fools*—thinking we need only lock up his strong room, and it would wait for us to come and examine it!" His hand moved to his brow and for a moment he looked so very tired, almost defeated, that it shocked Mrs. Pollifax. He was thinking of the lion deaths, of course, and now this mysterious burglary, whatever it meant, and she tried to find a comforting word and failed.

Kadi, seeing this, rallied to say crisply, "Whatever's stolen would have to be important, Sammy?"

"And dangerous in the wrong hands, yes," he said, "but what is most alarming is that whoever did this knew of the strong room and how to find it."

"How many know?" asked Mrs. Pollifax.

"Myself . . . Joseph."

"Police? The palace guards?"

He shook his head. "No one in *my* police." He hesitated, frowning. "President Simoko's police or aides, perhaps? Joseph, who among Simoko's people would have had access?"

Joseph shook his head. "Nobody, I swear. Only President Simoko came here, this I know, all the time I work in palace. It was known by us—that it be here—but nobody know which door, only President Simoko come."

Sammat nodded, and his moment of despair passed. Straightening his shoulders he said to Joseph, "At least not much was taken, you can see that. Someone was very selective, but until we examine what's here, and learn more—"

Joseph looked horrified. "You be chief! The *mbala* be found *now*! Punished! Given *mwabvi*."

"The ordeal poison?" Sammat gave him a sharp glance. "There will be no ordeal poison!" And to the sergeant, sternly, "No one is to hear of this, Sergeant Simakonda, you understand? I know of strong medicine that will tell me who the thief is— who the *mbala* is, *ona?*"

The sergeant nodded. *"Inde."*

Sammat said quietly, *"Zikomo,"* and to the others, "Shall we go?"

"But this is *udio*—evil!" sputtered Joseph. "To do nothing is—is *apiro!*"

"Is 'madness'?" repeated Sammat, reproachfully. "Come, come, Joseph," and he spoke to him softly in Ubangiban, calming him.

"As you see, I make many mistakes," Sammat said later, ruefully, as they stopped in the garden before parting. "I was careless, terribly careless."

"You can't think of everything," Mrs. Pollifax reminded him. "It's been only ten months since you returned, and you've thought of the *right* things. You've thought of people, not documents and old records."

"Yes, Simoko is the *past*," added Kadi, "and you've been thinking of the future, how can you call that a mistake?"

Once again Sammat's hand moved to his forehead to shelter his face. "Nevertheless Simoko was a ruthless man, I should have paid *attention* to the past. In spite of what I said in the strong room, to calm Joseph, something very important has to have been taken from those files to explain such recklessness. A guard checks all the doors, and always the door to the strong room, on every round that he makes, yet someone moved through that locked door in the hall, and then through the padlocked gate inside, like a *mzukwa*, a ghost."

"*No* ghosts," said Kadi firmly.

He smiled faintly. "It's more comfortable to think it a ghost than a fellow human being who can so easily—what was the word, *pick locks*?" He sighed. "I must call in Chief Inspector Banda and have the room checked for fingerprints." He said this but he didn't move. Instead he looked at Kadi and then at Mrs. Pollifax, searching their faces, and suddenly gave them a quick and radiant smile. "I find myself at this moment infinitely grateful you are both here with me. Joseph is my friend, but you see how quickly he reverts to the old ways, urging punishment by the ordeal poison."

"What is the ordeal poison?" asked Mrs. Pollifax.

"A suspect—which we do not have," he said dryly, "comes before a poison oracle—and I hope we no longer have any of *them*—and is put through a complicated ritual that includes a gourd with poison mixed in water. The suspect drinks the poison, after which the poison is personally addressed by the oracle, and if the suspect is guilty he dies. If innocent, he doesn't die." He went on thoughtfully, "It's quite unlike Joseph to suggest such a ritual. I had no idea he still subscribed to the old ways." He said abruptly, "But I must go, there's suddenly a great deal to do."

Watching him hurry away Kadi said wryly, "He forgets that Joseph didn't go to Yale."

Mrs. Pollifax said nothing. She was thinking that any enemy of Sammat's could certainly make good use of a dictator's secret files, especially if included among them was a list of informants and spies. . . . It was chilling to realize: President Simoko might be dead, but the people he had corrupted and depended upon were still very much alive.

7

The experimental farm, explained Dr. Merrick, occupied fifteen acres of once-barren land behind the palace. To Mrs. Pollifax it looked like a giant patchwork quilt of bright greens of varying shades and height, each square punctuated by white markers, presumably denoting what crop had been planted and when. A tall cistern fed a modest irrigation ditch that trickled past small earth dams, against a background in the distance of what looked to be fruit trees surrounded by chicken wire. Native Ubangibans in green aprons were working here and there. "Extension workers," commented Dr. Merrick. "Most of them will be visiting villages tomorrow to give pep talks and reports to the farmers, and hear what they think." Over by the fruit trees Mrs. Pollifax saw a cluster of farmers bending over an irrigation ditch, while a green-aproned man apparently led a discussion on its design. Next to the crudely built warehouse stood the greenhouse, but they were in search of Tony Dahl and there was no time for Mrs. Pollifax to see what was growing in it.

They found Tony in the warehouse inventorying sacks of seed. When he looked up and saw them his gaze lingered on Kadi with special curiosity.

"Oh," he said, flushing, "you have to be Dr. Hopkirk's daughter. Is your arm better?"

Dr. Merrick said dryly, "She ought to be back in the infirmary, stubborn child. She's threatening a visit to Sharma's son if she's not healed inside of twenty-four hours."

"Not to Sharma?" asked Mrs. Pollifax.

"He's turned over that part of his—should I say 'practice'?—to his son Chibambo now; he's a very gifted healer, too."

"But you haven't introduced Mrs. Pollifax," Kadi told him reproachfully.

"We've already met," said Tony. "Yesterday morning, in the public market."

Kadi looked at her doubtfully. "You were there?"

"Yes, but we're here now to show you what we found this morning," and holding out the circle of metal to Tony Mrs. Pollifax dropped it into his palm.

"Let's go outside in the sun," he suggested and they sat down in a row on the steps outside while

Tony examined the object, turning it over and over in his hand. "Where did you find this, anyway?"

Dr. Merrick explained, and Tony murmured, "Hmmm . . . leaden bronze, very delicate. The snake theme is interesting, especially since each snake holds an egg—did you notice this?—which takes us into the ancient belief among many tribes that this was how the world was born. I'd say it's a medallion of some sort. . . . One wonders if it was buried with the skull." He looked up at them with serious brown eyes. "It really does make one think. . . ."

"Of what?" asked Mrs. Pollifax.

"Of what else might be there. Of doing a bit of careful probing where the skull was found, I mean, to see if it's just a place where one skull and someone's garbage was buried fifty years ago, or whether it's a real find. This medallion suggests that it might be."

"Ah—we've snagged him," Dr. Merrick said merrily. "You know, of course, that you're the only one with the experience to do that kind of reconnoitering?"

"Yes, darn you, but I'll need permission," Tony said. "Quickly, too, because tomorrow's my day off, the only time I could go. Where can I find our busy *mfumo*?"

"*If* you can find him," Merrick said dryly. "He

was last seen with Inspector Banda heading down the hall to the storerooms." *To the strong room,* thought Mrs. Pollifax, exchanging glances with Kadi. "One of these days I'm going to tie him down and take his blood pressure, that young man collects a hundred worries a day."

"Well, we're all feeling rather pursued by demons just now, aren't we?" said Tony, with a pointed glance at Kadi's thickly wrapped arm. His eyes lingered on her appreciatively. "I'll go and look for him. Think there'll be enough gas for my motorcycle?"

"We'll steal enough from *somewhere.*"

Tony said shyly to Kadi, "Perhaps when your arm is okay you'd care to ride with me on my motorcycle?"

Kadi, glowing, said, "Oh I'd *love* to."

"That should be better medicine than either Chibambo or I can give you," Dr. Merrick told her. "Well—my day off ends all too soon, I've letters to write and the infirmary to check. Have a good evening!" Following Tony he turned to say, "Incidentally, Tony is a *very* nice young man."

It was Kadi who blushed now, and Mrs. Pollifax, amused, wondered if she had ever been so obviously admired before. Kadi had never mentioned having any dates at art school, but from the way Tony had looked at her she thought it possible this would soon be remedied.

"And get thee back to the infirmary," shouted Dr. Merrick to Kadi before he disappeared from sight.

Mrs. Pollifax, with a glance at her watch, realized that it was nearly four o'clock and that if she was to reach Cyrus by phone before his doctor's appointment in Connecticut at noon, she had better start the process at once.

After escorting Kadi to the infirmary she began to look for a telephone. What she found instead was Sammat and Inspector Banda talking seriously and in low voices in the garden. Pausing, she said politely, "Excuse me for interrupting, but have you made any headway in finding out who attacked Kadi on Tuesday night?"

Inspector Banda examined her with shrewd eyes, and then glanced questioningly at Sammat.

"It's all right," Sammat assured him. "This is the American who came with the authorities to Languka in April. She is clever at things, and can be trusted."

If it was given to Inspector Banda to relax at all, there was an almost imperceptible loosening of tension in his tight expressionless face. "There was a full footprint there," he said in a clipped English accent, "but unfortunately, before we could photograph and measure it, a workman blurred it, leaving only a heel mark in the soil."

"Oh."

"In any case that was Tuesday," Sammat said with a sigh. "We now have this entry into the strong room, discovered this noon. Inspector Banda has just completed dusting for fingerprints."

"And found none," Mrs. Pollifax said, nodding.

Inspector Banda gave her a sharp glance. "You say this, why?"

"Sit and explain why," ordered Sammat.

Mrs. Pollifax sat. "Because it was done by a professional. In several of my assignments for—" She hesitated. "For a certain government department in the U.S., I've come to know two such men who picked locks with ease, one an intelligence agent and the other a former jewel thief who's now with Interpol. I've seen them work. They would have worn gloves."

Inspector Banda, startled, gave her a closer look and frowned. "We have thieves and pickpockets in Languka, but no experts like that. In fact, in my entire lifetime I've heard of only one person here with such a gift, and that was only a rumor. You recall Philimon Tembo?" he said with an inquiring glance at Sammat.

Sammat frowned. "The name's vaguely familiar. If he's our man, *find* him!"

Inspector Banda looked almost amused. "I would have to make sacrifices at the shrine for that, he's been dead for years."

"He could have trained someone?"

Banda looked doubtful. "I could look into that, of course, but during the Chinyata and Simoko years—" He shook his head. "I'll make inquiries, but so long ago—!"

Mrs. Pollifax rose. "Sammat, where can I find a telephone? I'll pay, of course."

He said absently, "My office . . . Joseph's there. Next to surgery, second floor."

"Thank you," she said, and with a nod to the inspector went off to look for the office.

Joseph, it seemed, did not know the word for privacy, and perhaps in a country of villages it was unknown. He sat unmoving at his desk while Mrs. Pollifax struggled to get her call through to London, and then to the United States, and then to Connecticut, and as connections mounted she resented Joseph's presence and wished she dared tell him to leave. He was shuffling papers at his desk but she knew he was listening, and she found this oppressive. When at last she heard Cyrus's voice she joyfully shouted, *"Cyrus!"*

"Well, m'dear," he said. "Great relief to hear! You've learned by now what upset Sammat?"

"It's not much," she said lightly. "How are *you*?"

He chuckled. "Seems Mrs. Lupacik likes soap operas, too. Very interesting conversations we have!" He paused and then said, "You're not alone, I take it."

She gave a sigh of relief. "Perceptive as always. Definitely not."

"Then how's Kadi?"

"Well," she said cautiously, "she's been in the infirmary."

Cyrus's voice changed. "Kadi! What's happened?"

"A knife wound, a few stitches. She's up and around now."

"But not an accident, I take it? *Who did it?*"

"No clues," she said soberly. "It was in the palace garden, and at night."

He said impatiently, "Next time find an empty room to call me, damn it, I can only imagine what you're *not* saying. Nobody after *you*, I hope?"

"I've met some very interesting people and am quite well, Cyrus. Only five more days until your cast is removed?"

"So the doctor says," he growled. "I'll join you as soon as I can."

"Then Cyrus—" She stopped, aware of Joseph's eyes on her.

"Yes?"

Very softly, quoting Kadi, she said, *"Kàm kwík kwík, bo,"* and hung up.

She had not finished with her day yet. Heading for the infirmary to see if Kadi would be there overnight she found Kadi in bed with Rakia hovering over her.

"She do too much," Rakia said chidingly.

Mrs. Pollifax thought it more likely the race to the strong room behind Sammat and Joseph, and the excitement of a robbery, had tired her rather than the stroll with Dr. Merrick to the farm, but after a glance at Kadi she said nothing.

"Okay, okay, I admit bed feels awfully good," Kadi confessed with a smile. Seeing Dr. Kasonde making his way down the aisle between beds she said, "But why can't I go to my bedroom and stay *there*?"

Dr. Kasonde nodded to Mrs. Pollifax, and to Kadi said, "You are too much like a bird, you might fly away. You need rest, *mwana*. We can keep an eye on you here. You are Mrs. Pollifax?" he said, turning to her with a smile.

Looking at him she realized that he was the first plump Ubangiban she had met: her scrutiny met with a round black face radiating cheerfulness, round cheeks, and a short, rotund body under a long white jacket.

"I am, yes," she said, shaking hands with him. "How is she really, Dr. Kasonde?"

"Basically tip-top," he told her with a smile. "But one must recall"—his English accent was as pronounced as Dr. Merrick's, and she wondered if he'd been schooled in England—"that she suffered some shock, and she carries eighteen stitches in that arm. She was most naughty—under strict orders to return here from the bus to the south, and from the official opening of the mine. Her body needs rest to heal. We do not wish an infection."

"But how long?" wailed Kadi from her bed.

He smiled at her. "We will see in the morning. You feel a captive? I will bring you books to read, a magazine or two.

"Anci," he said, turning to the woman in the next bed, "you are ready for home in the morning?"

The elderly woman in the next bed nodded, beaming.

Mrs. Pollifax followed him down the aisle to the nurse's station. "Dr. Kasonde? Chief Sammat is busy, and tomorrow morning I'd like very much to find and visit the diviner named Sharma. Does he live within bicycling distance? Is he in Languka?"

He looked startled, and then his face relaxed. "Good! You are curious about our people? It would be a good thing for you to visit him."

"Of course I'd rather wait until Kadi can go and introduce me, but—"

He nodded gravely. "But you wish to consult about this attack on Miss Hopkirk, am I right?"

It was her turn to be startled.

"Very sensible," he continued. "He is not far. You bicycle down the road to Government House, and across the road from it there is a path. It runs past an orchard, a chicken farm, and then you reach a field and beyond this, where the trees begin, there is Sharma. He keeps to the old ways . . . a house of wood and roof of thatch."

"Thank you, Dr. Kasonde," she said with equal gravity, and with a wave to Kadi she left. It was five o'clock and she was remembering that she'd been awakened at five o'clock that morning for the trip south. She thought it time for an early dinner and a quiet evening in her room.

8

In the morning, when Mrs. Pollifax made her way down to the great hall, she saw from the balcony that every bench was filled and the floor alive with children, babies, and mothers. Rakia, rushing out of the second-floor surgery said in passing, "Free Vaccination Day at maternity clinic!" and at the head of the stairs she paused to call back triumphantly, "The first time—six months ago—only twenty mothers come!" Then she flew down the staircase and Mrs. Pollifax watched her difficult passage through the crowd to the clinic.

Following her, stepping around and over children, she negotiated her way to the cafeteria set up for the hospital staff, and after a quick breakfast of porridge and tea she walked around the building to the front entrance and extracted her bicycle from the rack. Pedaling down the road toward Government House she returned the greetings of two male

cyclists in business suits, and exchanged smiles
with a young woman on a bicycle wearing a flow-
ered dress and sandals.

Government House was still in the shade of
early morning. Next to it stood the gates of the police station, and beyond them the street ended,
blocked by military and police barracks in endless
rows. Crossing with her bike, Mrs. Pollifax found
the path to Sharma's and mounted her bicycle
again.

It proved a level, well-traveled path at first, skirt-
ing a reed wall behind which the peaks of thatched
roofs looked like shaggy lemon cones in the bright
morning sunshine. A few kitchen gardens grew beyond the wall, followed by a field of clay and
scrub, until eventually she saw a screen of trees
ahead, and the outline of two huts in among them.

She braked, slowly wheeling her bicycle closer.
At that moment, from one of the huts, there
emerged a young man in uniform, walking backward and bowing, hands clasped. She heard him
saying, over and over, *"Zikomo,* Baba, *zhikomo
kwambiri. "* A diminutive man followed him to the
door, barefooted and wearing several layers of
dusty robes that ended at his bony knees—a fierce-
looking little man with a circle of pure white goa-
tee at his chin. The man in the uniform hurried
toward a bicycle parked among the trees and pedaled away down a different path, leaving Mrs.

Pollifax and the strange little man to observe each other with interest.

She cleared her throat and said, "You can't be—are you Sharma?"

"*Heya!* The American," he exclaimed. His voice was light, lyrical, faintly mocking. "Come closer, come closer!" He indicated the bench next to the door of his hut, and as she put down her bicycle and approached him he called out, "Laraba, two cups of tea!" and to Mrs. Pollifax, "I am Kamuzo Sharma, yes."

"Emily Pollifax," she told him, sitting down beside him in the sun and noting that he, too, spoke clipped English.

"It is well," he said, "that my people now go to my son for charms these days, they line up at his door by the dozen, seeking protection against sudden death from the *mkambo*." He turned his head to look at her with soft brown eyes. "You are troubled, I see that. I must rest a little before we go inside, that young man who left, his soul is very sick. It is a sad story, it was necessary to do much work with him." Studying her face he added, "You have come a long way to visit our country."

"Yes," she said, "and to meet *you*."

He chuckled. A young woman in a bright blue skirt and white blouse brought from the hut a tray with two china cups of tea that she placed between them on the bench, gave Mrs. Pollifax a lovely smile and vanished inside.

It was peaceful sitting there and sipping tea. The bright sun filtered through the leaves of the trees, leaving lozenge-shaped dapples of gold on the earth; somewhere in back of the hut she could hear chickens squabbling. A scent of herbs sweetened the air, but seeing no herbs nearby she thought it must emanate from her companion-in-silence. Beyond the grove of trees a bird swooped low before returning to a cloudless, morning-blue sky. Off to her right the trees thickened, shading a growth of scrub that stood man-high and rustled a little now in the breeze.

Except, she realized with a start, there was no breeze.

She said abruptly, "I feel watched, Sharma, I *feel* this," and stared into the dark jungle of underbrush from which she sensed watching eyes.

Sharma didn't follow her gaze; he only looked at her, studying the tension in her face. He smiled and said gently, "There are watchers—and there are watchers. Shall we go inside now?"

She stifled a reaction of anger at his indifference, at his not explaining what he meant; perhaps diviners were given to vague and ambiguous pronouncements, she thought crossly, and then her exasperation was overcome by embarrassment, because from the amused glance he gave her she gained the impression that he knew precisely what she was thinking.

There was no sign of Laraba. He led her through one dark, cool room into another, smaller, one, its reed walls hung with marvelous objects: woven designs on cloth, carved masks, gourds, totemlike figures, stalks of drying herbs.

"You must take off your shoes and sit," he told her. "For you I will throw the cowrie shells." With a flap of his robes he sat down, and removing her shoes Mrs. Pollifax joined him on the rough wool rug. She had been too busy looking after Cyrus lately and had not practiced her yoga; the half-lotus position proved impossible, but she managed to sit cross-legged.

Sharma reached out a hand for hers, held it for a moment, and then nodded. Delving into a leather bag at his side he drew out an assortment of objects and tossed them across the rug. Holding out the emptied bag he said, "This is *ku-uzira*—to blow with your breath into it, please."

Intrigued, she did as he said and returned the bag to him, whereupon he picked up a colorful stick, twirled it, then put it to one side to begin studying the objects that lay between them. These were cowrie shells of varying sizes and tints, a few smooth, worn stones, a curiously shaped piece of wood, and several feathers. For a long time Sharma observed them until he closed his eyes and she wondered—it was quite possible—if he had gone into a trance.

Opening his eyes he did not look at her. He said gravely, "You are not here by accident."

This was interesting and she waited.

"Since coming here, already you have been very close to evil, but not knowing it. It has brushed past you, you have met it. . . . I see you have met evil before, but this time it is not given to you to recognize it, not yet. . . ." Again he was silent, and then, "You and Dr. Hopkirk's daughter have souls tied together like *chingwe*—rope—or what you would in the West call fate, and in turn Kadi Hopkirk is tied by fate to *Mfumo* Sammat, like *mbale* and *mlongo*—brother and sister. He is a good man . . . *uyu ndi maka nde mkabvu,* meaning in your language one who surpasses the rest, but I do not yet see him becoming king."

This was worrisome, and Mrs. Pollifax frowned.

Again there was silence, and then, "In your bag you carry metal—a gun? This is not good, you have better weapons. It would be wise to give it *at once* to the person you intended to have it. That, or throw it away. For you a gun is *wachibwuwa*—an enemy. Bad medicine, bad luck. Not *mwai*, not good fortune. I will give you a charm to remove its badness for you."

She waited, silent.

He said at last, evenly, "There will be more

deaths. . . . It is *nthende*, a sickness in the country. Only when the fever breaks will there be a healing, and no more sickness."

She said bluntly, "Who attacked Kadi?"

He gave a last glance at the cowries, and for the first time looked directly at her. "That is all," he said, and began to carefully gather up the shells and replace them in the leather bag while she watched.

"I will give you a charm," he said, rising nimbly, and walking to a wooden bowl he looked over its contents and brought her a necklace, a thin leather thong laced with feathers and shells. "Wear this," he said, "these have been given much power. To protect."

She hesitated. Looking up at him she said, "Could I give this to Kadi? Have you one for her?"

He shook his head. "No."

"But—why not?" she faltered.

He said gently, "Because it is you who will need protection. . . . Now I must rest."

She nodded and quietly left, wearing the necklace of shells around her neck but troubled and frustrated by what he had told her: so much and yet so little.

She found Kadi in the infirmary, dressed but sitting quietly on her bed reading *Candide*. She looked up and said, "This Dr. Pangloss is a real nut, isn't he? Sammy was looking for you."

"For me?"

"Yes, he wondered if you'd help, he's in the strong room, and Dr. Merrick wouldn't let me go. Do you know anything about clerical-type filing? Is it like the Dewey decimal system?"

"Not exactly," said Mrs. Pollifax dryly. "But why me? I don't know the language."

"That's okay he says. Most of the documents are in English." She suddenly smiled. "I'm being let out of captivity later this afternoon; no temperature, appetite back, no more wobbly knees. The final checkup's at four o'clock."

"I congratulate you! And now I'll go and see what Sammat wants."

The strong room was identifiable by a soldier standing guard beside its door, rifle in hand and a properly stern look on his face. Seeing her he opened the door and called out, "She be here, *Yanga mfumo*. The *mzungu*."

"Oh good," Sammat said, and a moment later he was escorting her through the iron gate into the cool, dim concrete vault. He said, "So many papers on the floor! I tried Joseph—him I trust—but he didn't understand how to organize, or what might be of importance."

She saw that two chairs had been brought in, with two small wooden tables on which documents were piled high. Sammat said, "Take that table on the left—I really appreciate any help you can give me."

"What are we looking for?" asked Mrs. Pollifax.

He said ruefully, "I have no idea, frankly. Something important enough for someone to want. Half of a report with the other half missing, a page gone . . ." He shrugged.

Mrs. Pollifax glanced at the slip of paper on the top of the pile she had been assigned. "This certainly is interesting, but not important, surely? Here's an order in triplicate for two Rolls Royces, one black, one white. One four-poster large bed of rosewood. Five pairs alligator boots." She whistled through her teeth. "This order comes to eight million *gwar!*"

Sammat said grimly, "Yes, but not worth robbing a vault to find. That, I think, can be tossed."

She made herself comfortable and began the process of sifting through the papers. A list of names she put aside for Sammat to see, but most of the papers were receipts and copies in triplicate of orders sent out for guns, ammunition, uniforms, a bullet-proof vest, an iron trunk with padlock, caviar, a hundred cases of champagne. The man had lived well.

She had nearly completed sorting them when Sammat murmured, *"Heya!"*

"What is it?"

"The name of Hopkirk—a report on them!" He placed it in front of her and leaned over it. "This is not in English, it reads: 'HOPKIRKS: known friends of rebel leader Willie Chiume . . .' I knew Willie," Sammat said in surprise, "but I never realized he was head of the Freedom Party. Anything on Chiume in your pile?"

"There are some names—" She pointed to them. "But what does it say about the Hopkirks?"

"May 6," he translated, " 'Dr. Hopkirk set broken leg of rebel-traitor Reuben Matoka . . . *May 10*: removed bullets from two members rebel group, M. Chona, E. Mutale. *June 3*: known to have picnic at Medicine House, party of six included K. Matoka, D. Bonzou, both known traitors. *June 11*: P. Msonthi seen entering Medicine House midnight, wounded after ambush, Mapira village.' "

"But that was his job as a doctor!" protested Mrs. Pollifax.

"And here," Sammat said grimly, "here at the end, in Simoko's clumsy writing—he was not well-educated—is the word *chherra*: set a trap."

"For the Hopkirks?"

Sammat nodded. "Where is that list of names you said you found?" When she handed it to him he glanced at it and winced. "I must tell you that the word *pha* means kill" and he began reading the list aloud:

Reuben Matoka . . . *pha*   Willie Chiume . . . . *pha*
Martin Chona . . . . *pha*   Ernest Mutale . . . *pha*
David Bonzou . . . . *pha*   P. Msonthi . . . . *pha*

"These men," he concluded, "were executed by—" He frowned. "By M, S, S2, Z and B." He looked thoughtful. "Somewhere—*somewhere* here—there has to be a list of names identifying M, S, S2, Z and B." He looked thoughtful. "Simoko's secret police were called the *Seketera*, meaning the Witchfinders, but the people called them simply 'the Death Squad.' "

"A code book, then?" suggested Mrs. Pollifax, riffling through the remaining papers. "I'll look for a code list."

"I will, too," Sammat said, and returned to his table to exclaim a moment later, "Here's more on the Hopkirks! '*July 2*: Mrs. Hopkirk seen visiting the home of Davidson Chona,' followed by a list all through July of Dr. Hopkirk patching up men Simoko believed members of the Freedom Party, and—oh God!"

"What?"

"On this list Simoko has scribbled 'Hopkirk: *mzondi*,' meaning spy." He shuffled through more papers, and groaned. "And here is the order of execution for Dr. and Mrs. Hopkirk, by X12, X2 and X8. On the last day of July."

X12, X2 and X8 . . . *Kadi's three men,* thought Mrs. Pollifax.

Sammat handed her the slip of paper, and—though she did not understand the language—she stared in dismay at words that so coldly and ruthlessly ordered the murder of Kadi's parents, their killers shrewdly concealed by numbers. But something about this slip of paper struck her as odd: it didn't have the weight of the others that she'd held, and she said, frowning, "This is a *copy,* Sammat. All the other reports and receipts and papers were in triplicate. The original order of execution's not here, it's gone."

Sammat looked over her shoulder. "You're right."

"The thief could have taken it, then?"

"There is no doubt he stole many things," said Sammat. "But why? If we knew who did this we might know why."

"And the letters X12, X2 and X8 each represent a name," she mused.

"A very very *secret* group with an I.D. of X."

"But their names have to be somewhere!" she said angrily. "What about the other file drawers?"

Sammat walked over to the wall of closed drawers and pulled out a few, one by one. "Take a look. Over here at the far end are President Chinyata's files—old. They must have been brought over from his palace and kept for reference. *His* drawers are labeled Taxes, Police, Army, Palace Plans, Receipts, Household Guards. . . . The British had taught President Chinyata order and system; he was a much more efficient and thorough man than Simoko, Chinyata's soldiers and police were fingerprinted and photographed. No hiding behind initials *there.* . . .

"Now we come to President Simoko's files, which take up most of the vault. Here are the empty slots for the three drawers found on the floor, their papers scattered."

He picked up one of the three drawers and showed her its label. "This identifies itself as Top Secret #3, the other two are labeled Top Secret #2 and #1. . . . A secretive man, Simoko—and these are the three drawers that interested our burglar."

"How are his other files labeled?" she asked.

He walked past them, reading each aloud. "Architect Drawings—Orders London—Orders Paris . . . Here are five drawers labeled Taxes, and so on. I've skimmed through all of them, and they hold exactly what they say."

She said thoughtfully, "There would have *had* to be a code book, and it's missing . . . a list of every member of Simoko's Death Squad, with the initial and number assigned to each one. And it's gone."

"Yes," Sammat said grimly. "There's something else missing as well, the names of the so-called rebels who made up the Freedom Party. We found only a report of six of them executed, but there would surely have been a list of everyone whom Simoko suspected. A complete list."

"So you think the burglar found both the names of the Freedom Party members—"

"—and those who survived his executions," put in Sammat.

"—as well as the code book identifying the men of his Death Squad."

He said grimly, "They're certainly not here. Three drawers labeled Top Secret have been virtually emptied and they are definitely and suspiciously gone. . . . Missing. As well as other secrets we can't even guess at." Sammat looked up helplessly at the towering files and then he looked at Mrs. Pollifax, and she looked at him, and neither of them dared to put into words the infinite possibilities behind what was missing.

9

Once the strong room was securely locked and the guard dismissed, Sammat said, "We must tell Kadi what was discovered."

"And not discovered," said Mrs. Pollifax.

They walked across the entrance hall, empty now of mothers and babies, and turned into the infirmary where a surprising scene met them. Kadi stood beside her bed in blue jeans, T-shirt and sandals. Next to her stood Tony Dahl, also in jeans and T-shirt, and at the head of the bed stood both Dr. Kasonde and Dr. Merrick.

Kadi, seeing them approach, called out eagerly, "Tony's found things! It's exciting! He came back early to show us. Look!"

A blanket had been spread across the bed on which a number of strange and interesting fragments had been placed, and it was at these they had been staring. Mrs. Pollifax glanced at Sammat and

saw that he looked blank. "The skull," she reminded him. "The skull the backhoe uncovered,
remember?" She thought it possible that he'd forgotten and she could sympathize with him because
she, too, found it an adjustment to shift her attention from the looted files in the strong room to a
discovery made the previous day.

Tony explained to Sammat, smiling, "I was very
careful, sir, I want you to know that. I borrowed
some planks of wood, and two men from your English foreman—I apologize for that—and we built
a small shaft at an angle to the skull, sifted every
inch of earth, and see what was found!"

Sammat said absently, "Oh, yes, you mentioned
your trip south yesterday to me."

"I've raced back," Tony said. "I'd like your permission, sir, to call or cable my archaeologist
friend Dr. Gibbons, and tell him about this. Look,
here's the broken lip of what was a good-sized pot
of coarse clay, and just see the designs on this fragment: wavy lines grooved with a comb, an ancient
technique, and see the tiny decorative circles below
it. Really lovely! Here's a stone bead, carved by
hand—glass beads came late to Africa, glass is
European—and look at this two-inch fragment of a
beaded copper chain, it could be part of a necklace
belonging to the skull that was unearthed. And of
course there's this medallion Mrs. Pollifax found,
and these other tiny shards."

All this was said in a great rush, with the patients in the infirmary listening in amazement to his enthusiasm. Only Sammat looked doubtfully at the fragments on display.

Dr. Merrick said tactfully, "He's worked with archaeologists, you know, if that's what bothers."

Sammat looked suddenly tired, as if wearied by still another demand placed upon him. "What is it you're suggesting, then? Because we can't spare you from your work at the farm, and I doubt World Aid would appreciate your taking time off for any more digging."

Tony vigorously shook his head. "No, no, I'm only asking if you'd mind my contacting Dr. Gibbons. He's in London just now, giving lectures. I can take photographs in detail of what's here and send them along to him, but cable or call him first. I think he might want to come and see for himself. And," he added, "it won't cost Ubangiba anything but a visa."

"Oh," Sammat said, relieved. "Well, by all means call, then, and take your photographs."

"The thing is, that seam of coal needed centuries to develop," Tony explained. "Those hills have to be remnants of marsh and forest formed aeons ago, the same that run through Algeria and produced coal in Kenadsa and Mazarif. If your 'gallery' of coal goes that far back in time, these objects could very well be centuries old."

Mrs. Pollifax glanced at Sammat and thought it ironic to be speaking to him of aeons when he was experiencing the uncertainty of what would happen in the next hour to his troubled country.

Kadi told him cheerfully, "Tourists, Sammy! A museum, maybe!"

"Yes, of course," Sammat said politely, and with a twist of a smile he left them to their newly found treasures, and the infirmary to its buzz of excitement at learning of Tony's discovery.

At the very least Mrs. Pollifax thought it a welcome distraction from four lion deaths and the knife attack on Kadi in the garden.

Tony had begun picking up the shards that he'd displayed on the blanket and was placing them gently back in his knapsack. "I'd better get back to the field office—there's a phone there—and call Dr. Gibbons in London." He smiled at Kadi. "You've an investment in this, too, want to come along? While I try to reach him I can offer you a rare, ice-cold soda to celebrate your discharge from the infirmary."

Kadi said, beaming, "That sounds great."

"You're not to overdo things this first day," Dr. Kasonde told her firmly.

Tony grinned. "I promise I'll return her in forty-five minutes because—unfortunately—I should be at Obosa village for that co-op meeting. Could have gone there directly, but first I had to show

Kadi what I found. And all of you," he added politely.

"Naturally," said Mrs. Pollifax. "And once re-turned, Kadi, I've something important to give you. A sort of present."

"*More* celebration!" exclaimed Kadi, and with a wave of her hand she made her exit.

Once outside and walking alone with Tony she found herself suddenly lighthearted and absurdly happy, a feeling only slightly reduced when Tony said, "I was pretty startled to learn you're not stay-ing until Sammat's coronation next month."

She said quickly, "Oh but I'll be back for it. I came this time—well, Sammat asked for help. Ex-cept I've so far not been of any help at all," she added sadly, "what with spending valuable time in the infirmary."

"But you *will* be back?" he repeated.

She looked up at him and smiled. "I cer-tainly will."

"What help did he need of you?" he asked curiously.

"A little detective work. Because he's in trou-ble." But she didn't want to talk about Sammat, or about leaving Ubangiba, not now, and she quickly changed the subject. "Isn't it exciting, what you found today in the south? If it's important will they let you take charge? Senior archaeologist and all that?"

"Whoa," he said, looking down at her and smiling, "archaeology doesn't work that way, and besides I've a real commitment now to World Aid. In college I majored in African history, with a minor in archaeology—and yes, I *thought* that might be *it*—but each summer I spent with Dr. Gibbons in Egypt showed me how tough it is, archaeology. To make a living, I mean. I had to save all winter to pay my own way to Egypt and back, and always came home broke."

"You weren't *paid*?"

He laughed. "You'd be surprised how many students are eager to work for nothing, just for the experience. And Dr. Gibbons has to spend half his time pleading for grants from foundations, or geological societies, or governments. I'm not sure I'm that dedicated. I've decided I'd rather teach African history one of these days, but I wanted to first really learn about Africa, live here, learn some languages. World Aid is great—lots of variety, something different every day, and what's more I'm actually paid for doing what I enjoy.

"But let's talk about something else," he said and reaching for her hand he held it companionably as they passed the greenhouse and headed for the warehouse. "Like *why* you have to go back so soon?"

"Oh—to art school," she told him. "I'm studying wood carving and painting, I've been carving for years. Esau Matoka taught me, he comes from our village—or did. You'll have to meet him, he's the best of all of them."

"I'd like very much to meet him," he said, and pointing, "Here's the field office."

He unlocked the huge padlock on the door and they entered a room whose rough-board walls were papered white with thumbtacked schedules, memos, maps, charts, and lists, the only furniture a small gas-run refrigerator, a desk, and three chairs. But the desk held that rare object, a telephone, and the refrigerator held several tins of cola, one of which Tony presented to her with a glass and a flourish.

"Have a seat," he said. "There could be a miracle and I get through at once to London, but if not, there's a *National Geographic* over there to look through."

Today, it seemed, there was a miracle because presently she was hearing words like rim section, transverse grooves, and bi-arcuate bosses. It sounded very professional indeed, and as she watched Tony's eager face, and how he ran his hand through his tousled blond hair, she was thinking, *I like him, I like him, if I'm not careful I'm going to fall in love with him.*

When he put down the phone he looked satisfied. "He was impressed, he'll let me know how impressed later."

As they strolled back to the palace, again hand in hand, they were both oddly silent. His motorcycle was just inside the entrance, chained to a post; she watched as he unlocked the chain and she followed him as he wheeled it outside.

Mounting its saddle he said soberly, "I really hate to think of you leaving even for a few weeks. I never thought I'd meet someone like you."

She said gravely, "I feel that way, too. I'm surprised."

He nodded and flicked on the ignition. "And if I'm not careful," he said sternly, echoing her own thought, "I'm going to fall in love with you."

With a roar the motorcycle sped away down the driveway, leaving Kadi to whisper, "But don't be *too* careful, Tony, please?"

"And now," said Mrs. Pollifax when Kadi was once again in the room they shared, "now at last for the gift, so to speak, that I was about to give you in the garden the other night. Which I certainly wish you'd had with you when you dashed off into the darkness." She brought the pistol out of her bag. "I've cartridges somewhere, too," she added, digging deeper into the bag.

"B-but Emmyreed," Kadi stammered, "where on earth did you get this? Guns are banned here. Surely Sammy didn't—"

"No, no, I bought it on the black market. Dr. Merrick told me where."

Kadi laughed. "You did that? He's a dear, isn't he, Dr. Merrick?" She sobered and said, "Yes, I do wish I'd had it that night, I was such a fool. You worried even then, didn't you? . . . and I—I've shoved deep every memory of those three men. You think the person who attacked me in the garden was really after *me*? And might be connected to that nightmare day?"

"Not necessarily that particular man," said Mrs. Pollifax. "You also glimpsed two other men, and neither of them wearing masks, either."

Kadi shook her head. "But I didn't *see* the other two men, only their backs as they walked away."

"Would those two men know that?" she asked. "Kadi, I don't think you've thought this through seriously. Or wanted to."

Kadi looked startled. "You mean—?"

"I mean," explained Mrs. Pollifax, "the one man who saw you need only have said later, 'the girl was watching, I saw her hiding in the tall grass, she may have seen *everything*.' Kadi, you can't overlook the fact that you may be a threat to someone. I've admired your common sense but in this situation you're blocking out too much, including the fact that you could still be in some danger if any of those men—X12, X2 and X8—are alive."

"All those initials! What are you talking about?"

"Sammat and I found the orders to execute your parents in the strong room this afternoon, Kadi. The killers were referred to as X12, X2 and X8. We couldn't find their names."

"Oh God," Kadi said.

"So here is the pistol. I'll help you make some kind of holster for shoulder, waist or ankle."

There was a glitter of tears in Kadi's eyes. She leaned over and kissed Mrs. Pollifax on the cheek. "I truly thank you for this, Emmyreed." Suddenly smiling through her tears she said, "And what else have you been doing while I've been stuck in the infirmary?"

"I've visited Sharma."

Kadi shook her head and said humorously, "And who told you where to find *him*?"

"Dr. Kasonde. Now shall we go down for dinner in the cafeteria? Dr. Merrick recommended a quiet evening with *Candide*, so that by tomorrow you can finally do anything you choose. Within reason," she added quickly.

What Kadi chose to do the next morning was to buy presents. "Something to celebrate my release from the infirmary," she said. "A present for Cyrus, and for you, and for my wood-carving teacher at school. I used to visit Esau Matoka and watch him carve little wood sculptures, he's one of the reasons

I carve now. There was Reuben Kanangu, too, but
he's several miles away. You'll come, won't you?
Esau's not far, just off the boulevard now, halfway
to the airport."

"Think you should walk that far?"

"I feel fine, Emmyreed, and I'd love to walk!"

"Perhaps Sammat would enjoy going with us?"
asked Mrs. Pollifax.

Kadi shook her head. "Too busy. Later this
morning he meets with all the tribal chiefs to talk
about the—well, I suppose the rumors and the murders. He wants to meet it all head-on," she explained. "I mean, it's only weeks now until he's to
become king."

"He won't be king yet." The five words had
slipped out without thought, and Mrs. Pollifax was
appalled.

Kadi looked at her in surprise. "Of course he's
to be king."

"Yes, of course," Mrs. Pollifax said quickly, and
thought, *Did I really believe Sharma, then, that
odd, fierce-looking royal diviner?* The question intrigued her. To be so exceptional a diviner meant
that, in Western terms, he was an exceptional *psy-
chic*. She had met psychics, and known a few—a
difference there—and she was aware that some
could be alarmingly destructive and horribly
wrong. Yet she realized that she had believed
Sharma, perhaps because she'd sensed no ego in

him, only a great simplicity. Nor could she forget
that, as royal diviner, he had predicted to King
Zammat ten years of evil following his death, and
Sharma had certainly been accurate, as well as hon-
est, about *that*. Yes, she had trusted Sharma.

But he had omitted explaining why Sammat
would not be crowned as king in a few weeks, and
this still worried her.

They began their walk up the boulevard, and
Mrs. Pollifax was touched by how many people
stopped Kadi to point to her bandaged arm and ask
how she was feeling. Strolling past Moses's bicycle
shop Mrs. Pollifax paused at the Bang-Bang Snack
Bar. "Let's go in," she said. "It looks surprisingly
American, and I'm thirsty."

The interior was indeed very American, with
Formica tables lining the walls, and plastic-covered
red seats. There was a dramatic mural on one wall,
and a long counter with two men in white jackets
dispensing food and drink. The menu, however,
was odd: there was barbecued chicken, chicken de-
luxe, fried chicken, and there was also goat. They
ordered a cola without ice, wary of unboiled water.

Sipping it, and facing the window, she and Kadi
were talking when Mrs. Pollifax glanced up to
see a man standing outside and staring intently
at the two of them. She recognized him: it was
Moses, but before she could lift a hand to wave
at him he had vanished. She said, "I somehow

had the idea he was a recluse and never left his compound."

"Who?" asked Kadi, turning to look.

"The man who sold me my bicycle, I just saw him outside looking at us through the window."

Kadi laughed. "How could anyone never leave his house? He'd have to buy food, wouldn't he?"

But there had been something disturbing about his gaze, and the intensity of it. *He was watching us,* Mrs. Pollifax thought, but without a smile, or any acknowledgment, and she wondered how long he'd been standing there. *Oh well,* she decided with a shrug, and finishing her soda she smiled. "Esau Matoka next?"

"Oh *yes*," Kadi said eagerly, and they walked out into the sun again, crossed the boulevard, and began looking for the street where Kadi's friend lived. It proved to be a narrow unpaved lane, shaded by trees and lined with fences behind which chickens pecked at the earth; the houses themselves were substantial, being of square concrete blocks with tin roofs. "A luxury," Kadi said, pointing to the roofs. "Expensive!"

Mrs. Pollifax felt that even she could have located the Matoka house because its door held wonderfully carved posts on either side of it, and in the center of the yard stood a tall, abstract pyramid of metal and stones. The house had been painted a pale blue, and there were beds of bright flowers: an artist definitely lived here.

Kadi opened the low gate. "He works in the back but I'll ring the bell anyway."

The bell hung on a rope beside the door. As Kadi grasped the rope and the first chime pealed it was accompanied by a thin scream. Mrs. Pollifax thought in surprise, *How macabre to have a bell that sounds like a scream,* and then abruptly Kadi silenced the bell, listening, and a second scream rent the silence, a scream of terror and agony, and without a word Kadi was running—running around the house to the rear, and Mrs. Pollifax was racing after her, fearful, her heart pounding.

He was lying in the dust of the path behind the house, one hand clutching a small carved figure, the other arm flung out across the earth. A slender man, the back of his gray shirt torn into shreds, his neck oozing blood that slowly stained the shirt, forming strange and intricate patterns.

It was Kadi who screamed now, and Mrs. Pollifax grasped her and turned her away, saying, "Don't look, don't look!"

"But it's Esau," she sobbed, "it's Esau!"

"Go and get help," Mrs. Pollifax told her. "Quickly, Kadi, go *fast.*" It was all that she could do to prevent Kadi turning over that still and bloody figure. "Hurry," she told her.

Sobbing, Kadi obeyed, calling out as she went, "Help! Somebody *help!*"

Mrs. Pollifax knelt beside the man, and without touching him studied what she could see: the mark of claws on his right cheek, the terrible marks on the back and the neck. She hoped that he was still alive but she doubted it; his mouth remained open in a silent scream, and groping in her purse for a pocket mirror she held it as best she could to his mouth, at a slant, but it told her nothing. Either he was no longer breathing or he would have to be turned over on his back to be examined more closely. She wondered if she ought to do this; police in America did not appreciate a wounded man being touched, but under the circumstances—

The sun was hot and the dust had scarcely settled from his fall to the earth. She realized that he must have been attacked at the very moment that she and Kadi walked up the path to his house, and this meant the killer couldn't have gone far. Where *was* help, she wondered angrily—did no one have a telephone here? Two flies had settled on Esau's bloody wound and she brushed them away. Glancing around her she quieted enough to observe her surroundings, and also to think. . . . Here behind the house, some nine feet away from her, stood Esau's workshop, its roof and three walls of thatch open to the sun, the interior in shadow. Behind this rose a thicket of vines and brush, at one point broken and flattened. *The killer came through to him from the rear,* she thought, staring into their darkness.

With a shiver she returned her attention to Esau and sat quietly, keeping watch over him, brushing flies away from the still and bloody body and impatient for Kadi's return, wondering why screams had brought no one, wondering where Kadi was, and for how long she must sit here alone. And once again there came over her the feeling that she was being watched, just as *she* kept watch over Esau.

I've got to stop this paranoia, she told herself, *this obsession with being watched, it's ridiculous, it's sheer nervousness.* Out on the street she heard voices at last, but at the same moment, off to the right behind the workshop, she heard the snapping of dried twigs. Someone was retreating in haste, and *oh hell,* she thought furiously, *it's not paranoia, I really* was *being watched, I was, I was, there was someone standing there all this time.*

The yard was suddenly full of people: two young men in police uniform, one of the men from the Bang-Bang Snack Bar, three curious little boys, and several women, awed and curious. There was the sound of a car and Inspector Banda came hurrying in, followed by Kadi. It was Inspector Banda who turned over the body, and after one quick glance Kadi looked away; Mrs. Pollifax held her while she was sick.

"Come, Kadi," she said gently, "leave it to the police now."

Pale and red-eyed, Kadi rose. Across the compound Mrs. Pollifax caught Inspector Banda's eye; he looked at Kadi and nodded. He would see them later. She guided Kadi out to the street and then to the boulevard. Impossible for Kadi to walk back to the palace yet; she led her toward the Bang-Bang Snack Shop—*coffee,* she thought, *unless they've something stronger*—but as they reached the snack shop a movement next door to it caught her eye. The gate to Moses's bicycle compound was just closing, and then was abruptly slammed shut.

They sat in the snack bar and everyone was very kind; the man behind the counter brought them hot tea and cold *mtibi,* and refused money. A young policeman drove up in a Land Rover, sent by Inspector Banda to find them, and he, too, was kind. Kadi kept saying "I'm all right, I'm all right," but she was white and trembling still, and the young policeman simply picked her up and carried her out to the Land Rover and drove them down the boulevard to the palace. Once there he said to Mrs. Pollifax in a low voice, "Inspector Banda say, ask Dr. Kasonde for shots of brandy and stay far away, they bring Esau Matoka here next. He speak with you later."

Mrs. Pollifax nodded wearily and wondered why on earth Sharma had insisted that it was she who needed a charm for protection when it was poor Kadi who seemed to be meeting one shock after another.

Again she remembered Moses saying, "Where there is *imfa*, there is no pity."

But why had Moses stared so strangely at them through the window of the snack shop, she wondered, and where had he been between that moment and the time when his gate closed behind him?

That evening she and Kadi returned to the yard where Esau had been murdered, and where now he was to be buried. Quickly, because of the heat.

"He will have been washed in herbs," Kadi told her gravely, "and a grave cut out of the earth for him."

Dr. Kasonde accompanied them; the yard was overflowing with mourners: family, friends, neighbors, elders, a priest. Inspector Banda was there, and she thought that she glimpsed Sharma.

Into the grave with Esau went his wood-carving tools, several carvings, and food and coins for his journey to the land of his ancestors. They did not stay for the completion of the rituals, but before they left Kadi stepped forward and dropped into

the still-open grave a small carved animal that Esau
had given her, and that she had brought to return to
him for his last journey. She was a very caring girl,
thought Mrs. Pollifax. As they left, Kadi said, "It's
believed here, you know, that the journey is very
short after death, because their ancestors live so
near to them, always."

10

There had now been five lion deaths, and Mrs. Pollifax abandoned the word *zitatu*, learning that in Ubangiban the word for five was *zisanu*.

After that, explained Tony Dahl, *zisanu* remained in place until number nine, but with accumulating additions: six, for instance, was *zisanu ndi chimodzi*, seven was *zisanu ndi kiwiri*, eight was *zisanu ndi zitatu*, nine was *zisanu ndi zinai*, but number ten was *khumi*, after which it began all over again.

Mrs. Pollifax said crossly that she didn't care to hear this, since she wanted no more deaths to count off in either English or Ubangiban.

"Fair enough," said Tony, "and anyway, what I came to you with is an invitation. Dr. Gibbons is flying in this morning from London before he goes home, he's just finished his series of lectures at Oxford. He'll only be here overnight, tomorrow he's

to catch the local plane from Agadir to Dakar, and
fly from Dakar back to London. Considering what
a dreadful day Kadi had yesterday—and you too,"
he added quickly, "I've been given the day off to
meet his plane and drive him down to look over the
site near that coal mine. It would be good for Kadi,
don't you think?"

"I agree," said Mrs. Pollifax, "and I must say,
your professor is certainly responding quickly! And
you've been given the whole day off?"

He grinned. "Isn't it neat? This time it's official,
World Aid is intrigued. After all, they're here to
help Ubangiba prosper, and if there *should* be
something worth developing in the south—besides
the coal mine—it would mean employment for
twenty or thirty men in the poorest section, with
foreign currency exchanged for *gwar*, food bought,
money spent. But where *is* Kadi?"

"Returning a book to Dr. Kasonde. Ah, here she
comes now."

Kadi looked her rosy self again—she had the re-
silience of youth and had bravely endured Inspector Banda's questioning of them both the night
before—but Mrs. Pollifax noticed that her eyes
held a sadness, a wariness that was new and would
need time to dissipate. Tony was right, though, a
trip south would be a happy distraction, and his
company even more so.

"He's coming so quickly?" Kadi said in surprise. "You haven't even sent the photographs, have you?"

Tony said modestly, "Well—he knows me, you see. He'll be here only overnight. He's just finished lecturing, and before flying home to Pennsylvania he'd given himself extra time in London to relax."

Kadi said skeptically, "I hope he can relax *here*." It was the only sign she gave that yesterday was still very near to her, and Mrs. Pollifax thought sadly that she had become just a little older today.

Tony glanced at his watch. "C'mon, his plane's due in twenty minutes, let's see if Mr. Zimba's brought the World Aid Land Rover yet."

"Dickson Zimba?" said Mrs. Pollifax quickly.

Tony nodded. "His job is with the lottery but this week he's been doing some accounting work for us at World Aid." He added ruefully, "For some reason we all take great care to call him Mr. Zimba. Wouldn't dare otherwise, there's something about him!"

Mrs. Pollifax smiled. "Yes, I've met him."

Dickson Zimba was seated stiffly behind the wheel of a Land Rover on which the insignia of World Aid was barely visible under coats of dust. With equal stiffness he climbed out, handed Tony the ignition key, gave Kadi a curious glance and Mrs. Pollifax a curt nod, and walked away, very erect and elegant in a black silk suit, white shirt and red tie. He must, thought Mrs. Pollifax, have *hated* delivering the Land Rover to Tony.

The plane arrived on time and Dr. Gibbons surprised Mrs. Pollifax. She had for some reason expected a tall and scholarly looking man, possibly very grave, possibly bearded but he was none of these: he descended from the plane talking over his shoulder to a man behind him, and upon reaching the tarmac he turned and shook hands with three other passengers, and—if Tony hadn't identified him—she would never have guessed this boyish, elfinlike man to be Dr. Gibbons. He was thin, his face was thin, his white hair thin, but there was a mischievous quality about him as he looked around him, extremely pleased at everything he saw, and curious as well. He was wearing polished loafers, chinos, and a shirt without a tie; he carried a tweed jacket and a trench coat over one arm, and an attaché case in the other hand. She guessed him to be in his late fifties.

Tony said dryly, "I have to warn you, he'll keep forgetting your names, he'll probably leave that jacket at customs if we don't watch him, and he's never been able to conquer his multiplication tables but I think you'll like him."

Seeing Tony, Dr. Gibbons rushed toward him,

saying, "Oh my, oh my, here you are, and with this exciting news! And you've found two lovely women as well. Both of you are Red Cross?"

"It's World Aid here," Tony told him politely.

"Oh yes, of course, of course. We can visit the site now?"

"Have you a suitcase?" asked Mrs. Pollifax.

He looked at her in astonishment. "I have, yes, so good of you to remind me. It has all my equipment in it—what I could fit into a suitcase, that is. And pajamas. You have the pottery shards with you, Tony?"

"Yes, but the suitcase," Tony reminded him.

"So good of you to remind me," Dr. Gibbons said, and once this had been retrieved, and his jacket, they set out for the south.

It was a pleasant drive; the Land Rover was too noisy for talk and Mrs. Pollifax saw far more than she'd noticed on the earlier trip. At this hour schools were in session—they passed two—and over his shoulder Tony pointed to the bush hospital—"really a hospice now for AIDS patients," he shouted. Dr. Gibbons sat quietly next to Tony, head bowed over the shards that Tony had handed him; occasionally Mrs. Pollifax saw him lift a magnifying glass to his eye; once the sun caught it, nearly blinding her. Tony had thoughtfully packed a jug of water, and another of soda, and there was a Styrofoam box under the seat that promised a fried chicken lunch. They arrived at noon, Tony dropping them off at the site where the skull had been found, while he parked the Land Rover under the shade of a distant tree. Nearly a mile to the west Mrs. Pollifax could see the tents and huts of the mining crew, the backhoe standing idle, but she could see the shapes of small children seated around it, still awed and no doubt waiting for it to bellow again like a dragon. Mounds of earth stood pyramid-like behind it, wrested out of the hills.

The trench that Tony had made on his first visit had been roughly filled in for concealment. Dr. Gibbons, observing the hill rising above them, murmured, "Promising, promising," and from his suitcase removed a trowel, a square of screening framed in wood, innumerable plastic bags and sacks, two cameras, and what looked like a miniature Geiger counter. By the time that Tony joined him, carrying a shovel, Mrs. Pollifax and Kadi had retired to one of the few bushes growing out of the hillside that was large enough to provide shade. There, she and Kadi unpacked the chicken and sat companionably eating while Dr. Gibbons and Tony postponed their lunch for reconnaissance.

But something worried Tony. "Footprints," he pointed out to Dr. Gibbons. "People have been here. Look—" He walked several paces from the trench that Dr. Gibbons was uncovering. "Someone's dug a hole here."

Kadi joined him to look. "Deep?"

Too hot and languid to move, Mrs. Pollifax called out, "There's another hole off to your right."

This captured Dr. Gibbons's attention and he walked over to examine it. "Anybody else know about what you found here?" he asked.

It might have been Mrs. Pollifax's imagination but she thought that Tony flushed a dull red. "Afraid so," he said.

"The entire infirmary," Kadi said, looking chagrined.

"Damn it yes," admitted Tony.

Dr. Gibbons nodded. "Nothing to be done about it now except praise the gods they didn't know *where* to dig—and let's get back to work. You, Mrs.—Mrs.—"

"Pollifax," she told him kindly.

"Yes. Keep an eye out for people."

The afternoon wore on; the sun moved across the sky, and fingers of shadow slipped down the hill to thin the rays of a blazing sun, but there began to be no doubt that what they had found by accident was proving to be a real find. The trench was deepened and extended, and its soil screened lest the smallest fragment be lost. It yielded excitements for Dr. Gibbons. When he rose at last, leaving Tony to fill in and rake over the trench, even

Mrs. Pollifax was excited. They had found a broken half of a curved and hollow bronze object, intricately decorated, that Dr. Gibbons thought belonged to a *siwa*, a ceremonial horn.

"Could be eighteenth century or older. Usually they're carved out of ivory," he said with satisfaction, showing it to Mrs. Pollifax. "See the hole for blowing? Rare! Other half may be in there, too," he said with a nod at the trench. There were also three more bronze beads that matched those found earlier by Tony, and fragments of bone now safely enclosed in a plastic bag. "Probably human," said Dr. Gibbons, beaming. There was also a small flat bronze rectangle with an intricate raised design. "Quatrefoils," he said triumphantly, and to Tony, "Dig up a shrub or two and scatter over the trench, once it's filled in. We want no more trespassers!"

"What now?" asked Mrs. Pollifax, as Dr. Gibbons removed his wide-brimmed hat and mopped his forehead.

"What now? I take these back to be tested, cleaned, examined, photographed, dated, and start begging for funds to really get something major started here." He looked wistfully at the trench site. "Hate to leave, hate to . . . We still know so little of Africa, you know. There's Zimbabwe, of course, and the excavations in Nigeria at Igbo Ukwu, but with so few written records it makes it vital to follow up every lead." With a sigh he walked over to rearrange the twigs that Tony and Kadi were scattering across the side of the hill. "Add a few around the holes someone dug," he told them, and with a glance at the sun, "Must, really must, see this chieftain fellow Sammat next. Introduce myself. Have a talk with him."

The four of them carefully inspected the site and agreed that all signs of digging had been erased. Packing up the chicken bones from lunch, Mrs. Pollifax waited with Dr. Gibbons while Tony and Kadi retrieved the Land Rover, and they began the long drive back to the capital.

In the morning Dr. Gibbons was gone. Almost, thought Mrs. Pollifax, as if he had never been there at all, except that he had left his trench coat behind in the cafeteria, where for several days it rested across a chair until someone removed it and hung it in a closet at the World Aid office.

11

In midmorning of the next day Mrs. Pollifax and Kadi set out once again to find a present for Cyrus and for Kadi's instructor at school. "And for you," Kadi added, fairly restored now in spite of the arm still swathed in bandages. "It's quite heavy, you know, all these wrappings," she told Mrs. Pollifax earnestly, "and so frustrating not being able to *bend* my arm. I can see how tiresome it's been for Cyrus with his plaster cast."

Mrs. Pollifax thought the circumstances not quite the same; a fall on glare ice that had been obscured by a dusting of snow seemed light-years away from being attacked in a dark garden by a man with a knife, but she amiably agreed to similarities. They would not walk far, she decided, and certainly not as far as the road where Esau Matoka had lived. "Let's see what the public market's offering today," she suggested.

"Good, it's different every day. And I've my sketchbook with me, too," said Kadi.

They strolled slowly up the boulevard on the shaded side, and presently Mrs. Pollifax learned that a visit to the market was very different in Kadi's company. The stall with the mysterious powders displayed on its counter was a magic shop, Kadi explained, the exotic ingredients having been pounded by a mortar into powder. The goat-skin that Mrs. Pollifax thought might be of interest as a small rug had not been properly dressed, Kadi said with a shake of her head, and would smell to high heaven by the time she reached home. Only skins dried and processed by Cecil Chimati could be trusted, if they found him. At the metalworkers' stall Kadi laughed and said the round metal bowls with tiny holes in them, handles, and short legs were not sieves, as Mrs. Pollifax had assumed, but stoves. "Charcoal stoves," she said.

"But how clever," murmured Mrs. Pollifax. "Of course! and so inventive." She considered one with enthusiasm. "Definitely I must buy this for Cyrus. Such simplicity! You know how he scoffs at all the complicated suburban arrangements for cooking out-of-doors." She laughed at the thought, and bought one immediately.

It was peanuts that Kadi bought, and they munched on them as they wandered up and down the aisles, but keeping the shells for the mulch bin at the experimental farm. "Nitrogen," Kadi said knowingly, and stopped. "Look! Violet Kamangu's here today, she makes glorious necklaces! Violet, it's me, Kadi, how are you?"

"Kadi! and the *njinga* lady! Hello."

"Njinga?" said Mrs. Pollifax.

Violet was beaming at her. "The bicycle lady!" She rose and shook hands with her but hugged Kadi, while Mrs. Pollifax stared at her, staggered by her beauty: the woman had the profile of Nefertiti.

She also had a tray full of necklaces fashioned of bone, shells, beads, glass and grasses. "But nothing of Esau's," she told them sadly. "A ring, and a *khosi* band he was to bring to me today to sell. And you, poor Kadi—the gourd cup is bitter, yes?"

"Very," admitted Kadi with tears in her eyes.

Mrs. Pollifax said quickly, to change the subject, "These necklaces are fascinating, and certainly unusual."

Violet, understanding, gave her a smile, picked up a necklace of carved bone and hung it around her neck. Purchases were made, gossip exchanged and when they turned to leave it was to find Dickson Zimba standing behind them.

"Mr. Zimba," murmured Mrs. Pollifax.

"You shop, I see." He bowed stiffly. "I feel I

was most rude to you on the bus, Mrs. Politflack. Just now, passing, I hear you speak of Esau Matoka's art? Please, to make amends, across the street in Mbuzu's shop I know there is one of his carvings, I do invite you to see. For you, Miss Hopkirk, Mr. Matoka was *tsamwambo?*"

"*Tsamwambo* and *tsamwali*," she said firmly, and translating for Mrs. Pollifax, "Instructor *and* friend. Do you mind?"

Mrs. Pollifax did not mind; waiting beside Esau's body she had glimpsed one of his wood sculptures in the shaded workshop, and trying to summon back memory of it, she realized that she might have been impressed if she'd seen it under less traumatic circumstances.

The Mbuzu shop, however, proved a longer walk than Mr. Zimba had implied, for it was down near the bank in a row of five narrow cement-block cubicles. There was a door, and one very dirty window with bars, and a sign: MBUZU'S. GIFTS. FURNITURE.

Dickson Zimba opened the door and ushered them inside and firmly closed the door behind him. They entered a long and narrow room made even darker by a door at the rear of the shop that had been left open to an almost blinding sunshine, and to a backyard that was barren except for a pile of broken chairs. As her eyes adjusted to the darkness

in the store Mrs. Pollifax realized it was empty of
Mr. Mbuzu. There was a rusty old safe along one
wall, a sofa in need of legs, three mended chairs,
and a counter holding trays of gaudy imported jewelry, but no Mbuzu.

"But—nothing of Esau's here," protested Kadi.

Only junk, thought Mrs. Pollifax, glancing
around, and she looked at Dickson Zimba. "Nothing of Esau's," she repeated.

Zimba's eyes blinked rapidly behind his spectacles; the glasses magnified his eyes, and he
looked—how *did* he look: embarrassed? pleased?
Abruptly Mrs. Pollifax realized that she and Kadi
were exactly where they must never be: isolated in
a room, the door to the street closed, and in the
company of a stranger who had artfully persuaded
them here . . . into a potential trap? She took a step
back, staring at him, and Kadi at once sensed her
distress and looked from her to Mr. Zimba and
said, "Go . . . We have to go—*must.*"

"Please no," said Mr. Zimba in a choked voice,
and then his gaze shifted beyond them to the open
back door and he looked startled. Turning to follow
his glance Mrs. Pollifax was just in time to see the
silhouette of a huge man outlined against the sun.
The figure filled the doorway, moved and was
gone, leaving Mrs. Pollifax to wonder if she ought
to be more alarmed by Dickson Zimba or by the

sight of Moses in the rear doorway, and then the front door opened and a black man in a brightly colored robe walked in. When he said, "Mr. Zimba! You be customer?" Mrs. Pollifax breathed a sigh of relief.

The moment was over, the shopkeeper had arrived but she remained shaken. Dickson Zimba spoke to the man in Ubangiban, Mr. Mbuzu opened the rusty safe and drew out a tall cup that had been carved out of a satiny brown wood, a full ten inches in height. The stem between the cup and its base had been sculpted into a marvelously carved and gentle face.

"Esau's work," breathed Kadi. "He's carved a ceremonial cup! Please, how much would you sell it to me for?"

"Not cheap," said Mr. Mbuzu, and a little bargaining followed, but not much because both of them knew that outside of Ubangiba the cup would be of significant value. It was delicately, smoothly, and sensitively carved, a true work of art, and knowing how little money Kadi had, Mrs. Pollifax entered into the discussion and added her own money to the deal.

The purchase was made, Kadi courteously thanked both the shopkeeper and Dickson Zimba, and they walked out into the hot noon sunshine. "But please," Kadi said, "what were you thinking

back there, Emmyreed? You looked, you looked—"
She fumbled for words.

Mrs. Pollifax could only repeat what had occurred to her at that earlier moment. "I realized we
were exactly where we shouldn't be, in a shop with
no shopkeeper, cut off from the street, and in the
company of a man—"

"Don't finish," Kadi said quietly. "I know what
you're going to say, it suddenly came to me, too.
How *could* we have been so careless! You really
think that maybe Dickson Zimba—"

Mrs. Pollifax sighed. "I have a lively imagination, Kadi."

"But he did have an awfully strange look on his
face," Kadi said, frowning. "Do you think he was
just embarrassed at no one being there? And then
came that spooky figure at the back door—a
giant!—I wish I could have seen his face, he really
did frighten me, but then he just disappeared. Did
you see him?"

"I saw him," said Mrs. Pollifax, and thought:
*Yes, and saw him two days ago staring at us
through the window of the Bang-Bang Snack Shop,
and an hour later his gate was closing after we had
found Esau murdered—obviously he was just returning—and all the time that I waited beside
Esau's body I was being watched. I know this because I heard the crackle of dried twigs and
branches when the watcher left.*

Had it been Moses?

Who *was* Moses? She had asked him this, and he'd said "Nobody."

She remembered that when she first saw his hostile glare and that terrible rope of scar tissue across his face she had nearly retreated from his gate. She had been tempted to flee, but only an innate stubbornness had insisted that she hold her ground. Yet after meeting him she had ended up liking Moses very much indeed.

She had always trusted her instincts but now Mrs. Pollifax asked herself which instinct she ought to trust, that first urge to withdraw after glimpsing him, or the warmth with which they'd talked later?

She thought unhappily, *Perhaps it's time now to ask how sane a man may be after being imprisoned and tortured for seven years. . . . I don't want to think it, but I must.*

She knew what torture could do to a person, she had experienced it herself at the hands of the Liberation 80's men in Hong Kong, but if she had endured it for only a few hours it had needed weeks—months—for the nightmares to end.

What might seven years of nightmare do to a man?

She felt a sudden, urgent need to call Cyrus and to talk of sane and familiar things with him, such as Mrs. Lupacik, soap operas, and whether it had snowed since the morning she left.

"Has it snowed?" she asked Cyrus when at last her call was put through to Connecticut.

"Emily," he said, "why the *hell* are you calling me from Africa to ask if it's snowed? Don't like the sound of your voice, either, you're in trouble. You alone now? Can you talk?"

"Guardedly," she told him, "but please—for just a few minutes *you* talk."

Mercifully he understood. He said there had been an inch of snowfall during the night, that Mrs. Lupacik was sure that in the soap opera "Time and Tide" the blonde woman named Winsome Aubrey couldn't possibly be a thief, while he argued that in his view anyone named Winsome couldn't be trusted out of sight; that Mrs. Lupacik had sternly removed eggs from his diet, and that in spite of the snow the daffodils were sending up brave green shoots in the garden.

"Is that mundane enough for you?" he asked. "Your turn now—speak!"

But Mrs. Pollifax had already received—quite selfishly, she admitted—what she had so much needed: perspective, and contact with a different, even soothingly mundane reality, and now she carefully edited what she had been going to say, aware that Cyrus felt helpless enough without adding worry to his circumstances. She explained more clearly what it meant in Ubangiba to be rumored a sorcerer, that in rapid succession there had been several odd deaths and that Sammat was becoming less and less his radiant old self. . . . Kadi had scratched her arm and there had been some fear of infection but she was fine now, and they had shopped for a present for him today.

He said gently, "Doesn't *quite* explain why you were upset a few minutes ago."

"I *was* upset," she admitted. "I was suddenly and acutely homesick."

He accepted this, at least she thought he did until he said, "May just have a word with Mrs. Lupacik about this."

"Mrs. Lupacik?" she echoed.

"Goes to Mass every morning," he said. "Must run out of people to pray for every day. Do her good to pray for Sammat and Ubangiba."

"Oh," she said.

"Kind of you to edit your copy, m'dear," he said, "but damn it, I can read between the lines. 'Odd deaths' indeed! Be careful, Em, you hear?"

12

Late that afternoon, while Kadi was helping Tony and the workers pick beans at the farm, Mrs. Pollifax walked into the office of the *mfumo* and asked Joseph when she might see Sammat. But soon, she added.

Joseph looked at her and frowned. "He be busy. Up at four A.M. today." He glanced at a sheet of paper in front of him on his desk. "Shipment of grain we buy out of Hungary come in. Mainza Mwango back from London—he be *fi*-nance minister, go to ask help for power plant. Many conferences! He be on *telephone* now."

"I'll wait. I hear the *local* phone service is quite good," she said cheerfully. "Does it extend all the way south?"

He looked at her curiously, as if he'd not expected conversation. *Perhaps people didn't talk to him often, with Sammat being . . . well, really quite charismatic,* she thought, *and Joseph without much personality.*

"Lines go to bush hospital," he said. "Now there be one line to mining camp, to Mr. Callahan, foreman."

"Yes, I see." She frowned. "Joseph, you work with Sammat—"

"*Mfumo* Sammat," he put in quickly, correcting her.

"Yes, but how is he really? Is he eating and sleeping well?"

"Pretty good," Joseph said stiffly, "but he work too hard."

"Yes, but these ugly rumors!"

He nodded. "Ugly, yes."

She was silent, wishing him more responsive, but—fresh from Mbuzu's gift and furniture store— she persevered, asking, "Joseph, do you think Mr. Dickson Zimba likes your *mfumo*? He is known to be difficult, or so I heard from comments on the bus the other day. He is not—not an *enemy,* is he?"

Joseph's face tightened. "Enemy?" He considered this. "He have *mapundi,* yes."

"*Mapundi?*"

He reached for the English word. "Inso-lence? Recklessness? *Mapundi.*"

The door to the inner office abruptly opened, and Sammat appeared, tall, serious and frowning. When he saw her his face brightened. "Ah, friend Pollifax," he said. "No Kadi? Then you and I will have a chat. You come at just the right moment, let's buy two American sodas from the cafeteria and sip them in the garden. Have I had lunch, Joseph? No, I don't think so."

Joseph looked disapproving but said nothing.

As they walked down the hall to the staircase Mrs. Pollifax said lightly, "Does Joseph disapprove of me?"

Sammat grinned. "I think this week he disapproves of *me*."

"Joseph? Why?"

Sammat sighed as they descended the stairs to the entrance hall. "One of the big problems in Africa is nepotism," he said, "and I'm determined to prevent it. Joseph is testing me, once again approaching me about a cousin of his needing a job. He's sure that he would do well as assistant to our future minister of public works when the young man, his cousin, hasn't even completed school! No, he doesn't disapprove of you." Reaching the cafeteria he insisted on paying for two sodas and led her out to the table and chairs beside the low wall of bougainvillea. "It's insidious," continued Sammat. "Very slowly a country's bureaucracy is overloaded: just one man's brother, father, uncles, cousins, and then it's his wife's relatives, uncles, brothers and cousins, et cetera, who want jobs. You multiply this by the hundreds, and presently *nothing* in the country works and nothing gets done.

"Ernest Bonzou is going to be minister of public works," he said firmly. "He graduates from engineering school in America in June, and he wants to come home, and I'm delighted! He'll design the power plant, pave the road south and create earth dams in the proper places." He smiled. "And he has promised me *not* to appoint any cousins, brothers, sisters, uncles, or fathers."

His smile abruptly disappeared, and he added, "If, of course, I am still here."

"There's that, yes," said Mrs. Pollifax, watching him, "which is why I asked to see you. Has Inspector Banda any suspect or suspects yet, have there been any promising leads, as they say, about the murders?"

Sammat's lips tightened. "About the murder of Esau Matoka, a few shreds from the lion mask were caught on the branches of the underbrush behind the workshop. They are synthetic—fake."

"The mask has been made by hand, then?" she suggested. "With local material that could be traced?"

"He hopes so."

Frowning, Mrs. Pollifax said, "But it's the motive behind the murders that interests me—as it must you," she added carefully. "It began after the decision was made that you be crowned?"

"Oh, yes," said Sammat. "Everything was going very well until then."

"Someone objects, then, to your increased power? You must have made enemies, you *must* know of someone you've affronted?"

He sighed. "It is a question I have time to ask myself only at night, when I retire to bed, which doesn't make for an easy sleep, so I continue very busy—and go every day to visit the shrine of my ancestors. But still I cannot name an enemy, and now there have been *five* lion deaths, and for all I know there is one occurring at this moment. Inspector Banda is as baffled as I, and he is investigating every day."

Mrs. Pollifax nodded. "You hoped that Kadi might circulate among the villagers and help, Sammat, but she's been incapacitated. As best I can, I've been trying to substitute for her."

She had startled Sammat. He said gently, "If Inspector Banda can make no headway—and he is very good—what can a *mzungu* do?"

"A *mzungu*," she said quickly, "can see what you may not, simply *because* she is a *mzungu*, and foreign here."

"You do not even speak the language," he reminded her.

She smiled faintly. "People are the same all over the world, Sammat: black, brown or white, we have the same longings, greeds, jealousies, hopes, triumphs, failures, loyalties, disloyalties, fears, anxieties, worries. Even a *mzungu*—an experienced one—can notice, watch, is not blind—regardless of language."

Sammat said ruefully, "Then I apologize. To see inside people is not usual, and from my years in America it seemed to me that a *mzungu* sees only our blackness of skin."

"That's their misfortune," she snapped. She would have preferred to ask what he knew of a man called Moses, who sold bicycles, but she was still shaken by the events of the morning and asked, instead, "What about Dickson Zimba, for instance?"

Sammat only laughed. "But I've told you—he's quite harmless, you know. He heads the Soto delegation, he's making a good record at the lottery, he will rise quickly to better jobs."

"He may not know that," she said dryly, and looked at him with exasperation. Sammat, she decided, was determined to think well of everyone, which might be an excellent attribute in a king but was certainly far too forgiving and inappropriate in a situation where murders kept multiplying, all of them thought to be by sorcery, and *he* the rumored sorcerer. Surely he was not unacquainted with evil, she thought, not when his own father had been assassinated. Could this be Dr. Hopkirk's influence, or had his father gone to his death with the same idealistic determination to think well of everyone?

She wanted to shake him and say, "Sammat, someone *hates* you—wants to destroy you, *remember?*" And then it occurred to her that perhaps he had known so much tragedy in his young life that he had survived only by suppressing memories, as Kadi had done, locking them into a room with a door he only occasionally dared open. He had opened it on the night of their arrival when he told them what had been happening in his country, but the door appeared to have been slammed shut now.

Or perhaps, she thought, what he was really suppressing was *fear*.

She rose, saying quietly, "I don't think I've contributed much to the 'break' you need. Do sit here and relax, Sammat, and thank you for the treat."

She would have gone directly to her room but, as she passed into the marbled entrance hall, she glanced through the glass doors and saw Kadi outside talking to Tony. He was seated in a dusty pickup truck, and if he planned to give Kadi a ride in it, she felt responsible to learn just where Kadi might be taken. She changed direction to join them.

Seeing her, Kadi said, "Tony's been worried about what he calls the 'dig.' Would you believe it, after work yesterday he borrowed this World Aid truck, drove south and camped out there for the night?"

Tony said, "Yes, and heard voices. I turned on my flashlight and scared them, they'd been poking around our trench. I saw three shadowy figures run away."

"But that's dangerous for him," pointed out Kadi, "and now he's leaving again to guard the site tonight. Do you think I could lend——"

She was going to mention her pistol, and to forestall this Mrs. Pollifax said firmly, "*No*, Kadi. . . . Tony, that's a long drive after a full day's work, why don't you speak to the mine foreman down there, explain the situation and ask if some of the tents the workers live in could be moved closer to the site? Originally he hoped they'd be there because it's closer to the well. There's no reason why a few of them couldn't pitch a tent there and keep an eye out for prowlers."

"Good thinking," said Tony. "Do we need an order from Sammy—I mean *Mfumo* Sammat—for that?"

Mrs. Pollifax considered Sammat's lack of interest in the site and smiled. "Try the foreman first."

Tony nodded and switched on the engine. "I'll reach the site before dark, so there should be time to move a few tents, platforms and all. Don't worry, Kadi," he said with a grin, "I was champion wrestler at college." He revved up the motor and drove away, leaving a cloud of dust behind him.

Kadi said sadly, "We should never *never* have shown all those shards in the infirmary so publicly. I suppose now *everyone* knows about them, what with—"

"—with news traveling so fast in Africa," finished Mrs. Pollifax dryly.

"Yes, and probably everyone thinks there's *gold* buried there."

"*Not* good," agreed Mrs. Pollifax, "but it's done, let's have dinner now, shall we? I'm hungry."

13

Kadi had enjoyed picking beans at the farm on Monday, but she had torn her blue jeans on a nail in the warehouse, and the next morning Mrs. Pollifax watched with amusement as Kadi sewed up the long tear with bright red wool borrowed from Rakia in the infirmary. The stitches on her arm were to be removed this morning in Dr. Merrick's office; it seemed ironic that she would now wear a matching scarlet gash down the leg of her jeans.

"You'll begin a new style," commented Mrs. Pollifax.

"Ha," sniffed Kadi. "I just wish I'd brought more clothes." She sat back and said thoughtfully, "You know, I do hope no one steals anything from what they call the 'dig'—such a funny word, isn't it? I mean, it's exciting to think what it could mean, especially for Ubangiba, if it turns out they find something really *important*. It would be horrid if anybody should dig there carelessly and steal what's there."

"Agreed," said Mrs. Pollifax. "Perhaps Sammat can be persuaded to send a few police or soldiers there to guard it?"

Kadi sighed. "He's so *feverishly* busy! I know he has to be, but he ought to be excited about a possible archaeological find, yet he isn't." She brightened. "Emmyreed, you know what would be fun? If the mine foreman moves some of his men nearer the road—to guard Tony's 'dig'—it would be fun to borrow another truck and go down and camp out in that truck for the night. Make a real picnic excursion out of it, and on the way back the next morning we could stop at my village—where I grew up—and I could show it to you."

"But first joining Tony at the site for a camp out?" Mrs. Pollifax said with a smile.

Kadi blushed. "I don't know why not. I wouldn't have to worry about stitches in my arm after today; we could sleep in the back of the truck and it would be quite safe, wouldn't it? I'd have my pistol and you have your karate, and in the morning, visiting my village," she pointed out, "I'd be doing just what Sammat hoped I would do: talk to people and *learn* things."

Mrs. Pollifax said with a twinkle, "Your mention of Sammat clinching the argument?"

Kadi knotted her thread, trimmed it, and said coolly, "To visit my village at *any* time we'd have to borrow a Land Rover or a truck, you know. What difference does it make when?"

This was a new Kadi, impaled by first love or infatuation, thought Mrs. Pollifax, and she briefly lamented the exigencies of being chaperon as well as guardian for a teenaged girl. It felt a long time since she'd gone through this with her daughter Jane but there had never been the complication, with Jane, of guarding her against someone with a knife and a propensity for dark gardens. Kadi was a darling, but vulnerable. Tony was older, well into his twenties, capable, and very nice indeed; they met on Kadi's turf; he could not help but find it interesting that Kadi was the daughter of revered and martyred missionary doctors. In turn, Kadi must be delighted to find a young man working in the country of her birth, who was drawn to it by a zeal not unlike missionary work, and who was also knowledgeable and more experienced.

The problem, thought Mrs. Pollifax, was how to guard Kadi without imprisoning her, and she found herself wishing that Dr. Gibbons would hurry along his report on the objects he'd taken away with him. If they were of no value then there would be no attraction from looters to the site, and if they proved of value then Sammat would certainly have to post official security guards with guns, or have a fence built around the site.

Choosing a neutral subject while she thought about this she said, "In any case it's high time you find out what friends in your village are feeling and saying about Sammat."

Kadi nodded. "Rakia was there on Saturday. She lives *here* now, of course—they moved to the capital soon after I left the country—but her parents and the rest of her relatives are still back in the village, and she visits them once a month. Takes food to them, and clothes."

"Has she said how they're reacting to rumors that Sammat's behind these murders? Are they turning against him?"

"The rumors trouble them," Kadi acknowledged. "It's hard for them. Sorcery is a terrible thing but Sammy's the grandson of King Zammat, and superstitious they may be but King Zammat was really loved. Oh, he was regal, but so *kind*. Wise, too."

"Did you know him?" Mrs. Pollifax asked, curious.

"Only when he was already old—to me at least—when he was much less formal. I'm told he used to be very remote and only rarely left the royal compound. He 'held to the old ways,' as my father put it, in spite of having gone to university in

England. Sammy thinks he loosened up as he grew older because of his books. He had this wonderful library, you see. But I think he must always have wanted to be more—well, more contemporary. After all, it's he who negotiated Ubangiba's independence from the British." She giggled. "It was about that time that he rode a bicycle up the boulevard and back."

"Did *what*?"

"Rode a bicycle. It really startled everyone, but in a way it sort of liberated them and they loved him for it. He did it on purpose. He was involved in negotiations with an English company to move here and build their bikes. He even sent three men to London to learn how they're built." She sighed. "Unfortunately nothing came of it, but the company did open up an outlet here for a while to sell them, and at least the three men sent to London learned how to repair them. Everyone who could afford a bicycle bought one, and the king gave away hundreds to people who couldn't." She was silent and then, "A king, you know, has always been the heart and the soul of the country. It's why the people—in my village at least—are very disturbed and don't know what to think." She added sadly, "But I don't know how long it will be before the rumors win and they turn on him, or riot. I can't believe they'd *kill* Sammy," she said, "not when he's the last of the royal line!"

Mrs. Pollifax thought, *Yes, and we must soon leave the country; there will still be deaths, and it takes only one person to assassinate a chief or a king, and it will surely be the man who hides behind a lion mask.*

Kadi gave her a pleading glance. "But what about the overnight camping trip?"

Mrs. Pollifax sighed, thinking how natural a picnic and a camping trip would be in the United States, but for Kadi— and in Ubangiba? She said carefully, "I have nothing against such an expedition, Kadi, but I have to add one stipulation. No, don't look at me like that, I quite sympathize with your having spent two of our eight days here in the infirmary, but it would be foolhardy to go without added protection. If Sammat will assign a soldier or two, or a pair of armed and trustworthy men— only then."

"For just a simple camping trip!" protested Kadi.

Mrs. Pollifax said tartly, "Nothing is simple just now in Ubangiba. Think of Esau, Kadi. And this," she added, leaning over and touching her bandaged arm.

Kadi turned to face her. "I'm sorry," she said contritely. "I wasn't thinking, was I. It's just that I so wanted—"

"—to be young," said Mrs. Pollifax, smiling. "I understand. So have your stitches removed and then talk to Sammat, and who knows, he might even like to go, too, it would be just the change he needs."

It was possible that Sammat felt a twinge of guilt at refusing to accompany two guests that he'd personally invited to his country. With apologies he told Kadi that he was too busy to join them for an overnight trip but he agreed at once to assign two armed security guards, Bristol Tanko and Roy Siwale, to accompany them.

After joyfully telling Mrs. Pollifax this news, Kadi raced off to the experimental farm to politely ask Tony what he'd found at the site last night, and to enthusiastically bring up the possibility of their joining him for an overnight camp out, with two security men to guard them. While she was gone Mrs. Pollifax put in a call to Cyrus, borrowing Joseph's office again but this time his presence was of no concern: she wanted only to learn of Cyrus's visit to the doctor, and whether he had shed his cumbersome plaster cast, and when he could join her in Ubangiba.

This time her call went through quickly, although the connection was poor, and Cyrus's voice muffled. "Cast's off!" he announced in triumph.

"And you found a leg there, after all?" she teased. "Cyrus, I'm so glad, when can you travel?"

"Damn it, not for a few more days," he growled.

"Muscles flaccid, he tells me. Stupid word. Checked it in the dictionary, it says 'weak and ineffective.' Might as well have said flabby. Three days of intense physical therapy ahead."

"Flaccid or not, can you walk?"

"Gingerly. No problem here, just a doctor who envisions me falling flat in every airport. Not coming home yet, I take it?"

She winced. "Not quite yet. Kadi—Kadi isn't ready yet, so—"

"Right." She could picture him nodding his head. "This is Tuesday. I'll make reservations today and hope to be on the Monday flight into Languka. I'll call later to confirm."

She wondered what to say until, brightening, she confided that an overnight camping trip was being planned. This sounded carefree and innocent—she only wished it felt so— and on that note their conversation ended. She hung up, relieved that Cyrus hadn't noticed anything in her voice that suggested worry. On the other hand, she noted that he had taken great pains not to mention Mrs. Lupacik's prayers at Mass for Sammat, nor had he brought up the "odd deaths" to which she'd lightly referred on the previous call. He'd not inquired about Kadi, either, and this was suspect. *He guesses,* she thought, *guesses but doesn't know, and is hurrying now to arrive here and learn for himself what's been happening.*

Nevertheless, she found that she regretted their bland and guarded conversation.

While she had been closeted in Joseph's office to call Cyrus, she found that decisions and plans had been quickly made. Tony was going to steal half a day from his weekly day off, and they were to leave for the south tomorrow, Wednesday, after lunch. They would go in two pickup trucks loaded with bedrolls and sleeping bags, and picnic dinners for themselves and the two guards, and they would experience a very American camping trip, returning Thursday to Languka by nine o'clock in the morning.

Tony would also, at the last minute, add a volleyball.

Mrs. Pollifax would remember that volleyball for a very long time.

14

The two guards, Roy and Bristol, were cheerful young men drawn from Sammat's palace guard. Each had been well-trained—and recently—in the military school of a neighboring country, Tony said, and being posted at the palace they knew Tony and had an easy, bantering relationship with him. Introduced to Kadi, Mrs. Pollifax was touched by their respect, even awe, at meeting her, and she realized that Dr. and Mrs. Hopkirk had become icons among even those too young to have known them. She felt that it must go beyond their martyrdom. After all, refusing a life of ease, they had spent over twenty years in this country healing, learning and teaching, and they had died here, which surely made them as native as the Ubangibans who had also been sacrificed to dictators' paranoia and ambitions.

Rakia personally brought the Styrofoam hampers

of food from the hospital kitchen to the truck, reminded Kadi to be careful, and gave Mrs. Pollifax a questioning glance.

Mrs. Pollifax nodded. "Yes, she is well protected, as you can see."

Blankets and bedrolls were piled in the back of the two pickup trucks. Mrs. Pollifax was given a seat next to Roy, who would drive the first truck, while Kadi rode next to Tony in the second truck, with Bristol in the rear among the bedrolls, rifle in hand. They set out at a time of afternoon heat that stilled nearly every sign of life: the leaves on the trees hung limp, there were few people on the road south, and only the Languka bus passed them, raising the usual dust behind it. Yet, if the air was oppressively heavy and still, it also held captive the fragrance of charcoal cooking fires, of hot earth and the sounds of birdsong, and brought a pleasant languor.

It was half past three when they reached their destination and parked in the shadow of the hills. Across the treeless barren strip of land they could see the backhoe shining in the sun and figures moving around it. Whatever villages existed in the neighborhood, they were hidden behind the woods that rimmed the broad field lying at the base of what Kadi called Tony's "dig." They parked; they were here, after all, to guard the dig as well as to picnic.

A fire was kindled and Tony produced a grill on which chicken could be cooked; Bristol had brought millet flour, ready to mix with water and bake overnight in the ashes of the fire. There was sweet beer—*mtibi*—and colas, and Kadi had produced a miracle: a tin of smoked oysters on which they nibbled while the fire grew hot. They inspected the "dig" and Mrs. Pollifax noted how wistfully Tony stared at it and how regretfully he left it. "You want to dig more," she said, smiling.

"Gets in your blood," he admitted. "At least nobody's visited it today. Apparently they come only at night, when it's dark."

"And if they're seen tonight?" she inquired.

He grinned. "One of the World Aid chaps brought back from his leave some firecrackers from the American Fourth of July. I stole one, just in case. Should scare the heck out of them, or so I hope—a rocket zooming over their heads!"

"Ingenious!"

Kadi said earnestly, "Oh there's so *much* ingenuity here, it always surprises—wonderful drums are made of goatskin stretched taut, guitars fashioned out of calabashes and wire, rattles out of seeds inside a gourd, and you should have seen the tortoiseshell masks my parents were given! Nothing is wasted, everything's used: dried, cooked, carved, or shaped into containers, hair combs, cups, whistles . . ."

After which she added with a grin, "I'm hungry, how soon do we eat?"

Ignoring the chicken roasting on the fire they reached into the hamper for sandwiches—*sangwìs* in pidgin, laughed Kadi—and sat on bedrolls in the truck.

"In one hour be dark," said Bristol, glancing at the sun.

Tony dug among the blankets and brought out the volleyball. "We can kick this around," he said, gesturing toward the expanse of field around them.

This was received with enthusiasm; they climbed down from the truck, and from his bag of tricks Tony produced a fold-up camp stool for Mrs. Pollifax, and after inspecting the ground for scorpions or snakes he set it up for her.

"Soccer?" asked Roy.

Tony pointed to Kadi's bandaged arm. "We kick the ball, okay?"

They agreed and formed a circle that gradually expanded, the four of them making a great deal of youthful noise, Kadi kicking the ball to Bristol, and he to Roy, and Roy to Tony. Mrs. Pollifax watched from the sidelines as they missed the ball, raced after it, kicked and laughed. Their shouts brought attention, and presently half a dozen of the mining crew, all Ubangibans, wandered down to watch.

Seeing them Kadi called out, "Want to play, too?"

This met with sheepish grins. To resolve the situation, Kadi kicked the ball toward them, and running down the field toward the woods she turned and lifted both arms to describe a circle.

Tony shouted, "Yes—spread out! Come play kick-the-ball!"

They understood. With enthusiasm they formed a great circle and the ball shot back and forth from one side to another with much laughter, while Mrs. Pollifax watched with pleasure.

Callahan, strolling down to see what was happening, commented, "They're a good lot of men, I've 'ad worse, I can tell you. The girl yours?"

Mrs. Pollifax glanced toward Kadi, where she had established herself near the woods; she could wish that Kadi was not at such a distance from her and from the guards, but a young man from Callahan's crew was not far away from her and seemed attentive. As she watched, the ball came rushing toward Kadi and she kicked it away, laughing. Mrs. Pollifax heard her neighbor shout, "Good show!"

"Kadi's a good friend, she grew up in Ubangiba," she told Callahan, and winced as the ball hit one of the players on the head, which met with fresh shouts of laughter. "But it will soon be dark, I think they should stop." Already she could see a pale crescent moon in the darkening sky. She glanced again toward Kadi and was startled to see no sign of her. Her eyes moved quickly around the field looking for her, and she felt a first clutch of fear.

"Where's Kadi?" she called to Tony.

He turned toward her, laughing, until he saw the expression on her face.

Holding up a hand he shouted to the players to stop the game, but already Mrs. Pollifax was running across the field, frightened now because the light might be dimming but it was still light enough to see that Kadi had vanished. *Oh my God,* she was thinking, *oh my God* . . . To the young man who had called "Good show!" she cried, "Where is she? Where's Kadi?"

Hearing only her panic, he looked bewildered.

Tony, catching up with her, said more calmly, "What's your name?"

"Jacob Bwanausi."

"Jacob, the girl—Kadi—where has she gone?"

Callahan, panting up behind them, spoke to the young man in pidgin English. "*Bèbi!* Young woman! *Hùsay?*"

Jacob replied with dignity. "I see her turn—" He turned, too, to face the trees. "I think somebody must call her maybe, I don't know. She go thus—" He pointed toward the woods, and to demonstrate he walked quickly to the edge of the field to look in among the trees. "I hear her call out—in very happy voice—'Philimon, it's really *you?*' Then ball is kicked to me, and—" He returned to where he had stood before. "I kick it to Willie. When I look back she be gone. This be all I know."

"A *happy* voice?" echoed Mrs. Pollifax.

Jacob nodded. "This I hear. She sing it like a song."

"She can't be far," gasped Tony. "Callahan, can we borrow your men?"

"You already 'ave 'em," he said dryly, and shouted orders.

But it was Mrs. Pollifax who led the way, preceding even Tony, and repeating over and over to herself what Jacob had said, that Kadi's voice had been happy at the sight of whomever she'd seen, but where was she now, and who on earth was Philimon, and if he was not dangerous to her then why had he been hiding in the woods, and if Kadi hadn't wanted to go, why hadn't she used the gun she wore in the ankle holster they'd so carefully made?

In spite of her frightened thoughts her experienced eye was noting how the tall grass had flattened to form a path: *someone* had walked here to the field and watched them playing and had made himself known to Kadi. But Kadi would never *never* go with a stranger. Why had she trusted the man who had called to her, didn't she realize that even someone she knew could be dangerous?

Something was terribly wrong.

The path disappeared as the trees thickened and

the grass grew short; eventually, after pushing their way through the underbrush, they met with a rutted thread of a road. It was here that the last of the sun's rays vanished and they stood in darkness.

Jacob, pointing to the left, said, "That go to village, other way to main road Languka."

Bristol said, "I'll go to the village, I know it."

Tony nodded. "Good, and Jacob and I will try the main road."

They rushed away in opposite directions but Mrs. Pollifax turned to Callahan and said quietly, "What I want is a telephone—fast! You have one, I hear? Please—a call to Inspector Banda, to the police, to Languka, to the palace, anywhere."

Callahan produced a flashlight and led the way back, with Mrs. Pollifax and the remaining men behind her. Once through the woods there was the mile-long walk at a fast pace to Callahan's trailer but it found Mrs. Pollifax tireless: *adrenaline,* she thought, and blessed it. The mining crew dispersed to their huts and tents and Mrs. Pollifax was ushered into Callahan's trailer. She saw only the telephone.

Callahan at once reached for it and waited. Soon he looked puzzled, and then he frowned. "I hear nothing," he said. "Phone's dead."

"There should be an operator?"

He nodded. "Goes through the army barracks' switchboard in Languka; they do the connecting.

Damn fools," he growled. "They set it up two weeks ago for me, and already it's not working."

She said quietly, "Or the line's been cut."

He stared at her. "That would mean the girl's disappearance was *planned*? What the 'ell's going on?"

Bluntly Mrs. Pollifax told him. "You saw her bandaged arm," she concluded, and lifted her hand to rub a forehead that was already knotted in worry and bewilderment.

Callahan moved to the kitchen, and returned with a full glass. "'Ave a shot of brandy, you look bloody awful. And sit down, missus, before you fall down."

She gave him a faint smile but shook her head. "A little brandy, yes, but sit no. I've got to find her . . . get back to the capital."

He nodded. "'Op in my Land Rover and I'll drive you down to the pickup truck, no more 'iking around for you, missus. Come along now."

"Yes," she said, and then, "But *why*—how could Kadi, after all that's happened, how could she—" She stopped. "Sorry."

They found Tony standing beside the truck. "Any news?" he called.

"Mr. Callahan's phone is dead," she told him. "We've got to get to the police, Tony—to Languka."

Shocked, he said, "You couldn't call the police, then?"

"No."

Grimly he said, "Hop in, let's *go*."

Calling a thank-you to Mr. Callahan, she climbed into Tony's pickup truck, both of them aware as they drove along of the empty space on the seat between them that could have held Kadi. Mrs. Pollifax's thoughts veered from an anguished *Kadi, how could you!* to a furious *And why on earth did I ever allow this disastrous excursion to the south!*

It was a sleepless night. She and Tony waited with a stunned Sammat in Inspector Banda's office, while in another part of the police station Jacob Bwanausi was questioned over and over again. Hours later, past midnight, the three of them drove back to the palace, made tea and coffee in the deserted cafeteria and carried their cups to Sammat's office where they sat, saying little but drawing comfort from each other's presence. *Like a wake,* thought Mrs. Pollifax wretchedly, each of them trying not to think what might be happening to Kadi and whether they would see her again alive.

Certainly Inspector Banda had refused Mrs. Pollifax even the small comfort that Kadi could have gone willingly with her abductor, or even have known him. "She had a gun," Mrs. Pollifax had pointed out drearily. "But no time to use it— always the case," he'd replied, and to emphasize his viewpoint he had efficiently ticked off the reasons that Kadi would not have gone willingly: first, the woods at that hour would have been too shadowed to clearly see whoever had called to her; second, there must have been only a resemblance to someone known; and third, "Miss Hopkirk struck me as an intelligent young woman," he said, "and having already experienced an attack in the palace garden she would be very aware of danger.

"To put it bluntly," he'd added, "why would she consider for a moment leaving you and Mr. Dahl, when she was having a very good time on a picnic she herself had planned?"

This, of course, was unanswerable, and by midnight the three of them had exhausted every possible theory and argument, and now they could only sit in Sammat's office and wait. Jacob Bwanausi's story had remained unshaken. "Her voice was happy. Surprised," he had repeated again and again, but they had only his word for this.

And who was Philimon?

Around three in the morning their vigil was interrupted by Joseph, and they roused somewhat at his arrival; he had just heard of this terrible news, he said.

"What do they think?" he demanded. "Who could have done this? Inspector Banda be good man, he must—*must!*— know who do this."

"He doesn't," Sammat said wearily.

"But what be he doing? What plans he make? He *must* be finding who did this!"

He seemed genuinely upset and Mrs. Pollifax appreciated his concern but she thought his faith in Inspector Banda something she did not share at this moment. She also wished Joseph would calm down or go away; his excited questions were quite unlike him, until she recalled his emotional outburst over the strong room having been burgled. This time, however, Sammat had no words to divert him, and only looked at him blankly, until Mrs. Pollifax held out her empty cup and asked Joseph if he'd mind bringing fresh coffee from downstairs. The silence following his departure was a great relief.

At dawn Inspector Banda came in his Land Rover with Jacob Bwanausi to pick up Mrs. Pollifax: they were both to be taken south to show him precisely where Kadi had vanished. Tony left for the experimental farm, grateful to have work to do, he said; and Joseph reminded Sammat that he had appointments today.

Obviously life had to go on.

It was a long, hot drive south, and in spite of the potholes in the road over which they bounced Mrs. Pollifax fell asleep, welcoming its oblivion. Once at the site, the next hours seemed unending. Each of the kick ball players was questioned; the corner of the field where Kadi had stood during the game was established and marked, after which Jacob was excused, to return to the day of physical labor waiting for him at the mine. Mrs. Pollifax waited under a tree, fanning herself, while Inspector Banda combed the woods looking for footprints or signs of violence. He found nothing. After this he drove out to the main thoroughfare and turned up the road leading to the nearby village, and again Mrs. Pollifax waited, this time in the Land Rover, reinventing all her previous images of hell. It was very hot, and the huts virtually hovels; the trees were red with dust, and the fields here looked thirsty and nearly barren. Chickens and small children crossed and recrossed the road; an old man sat on a bench smoking a pipe and watching her. When Inspector Banda returned from questioning the elders, however, he had learned one small thing at last.

"They tell me a very old truck was parked at the side of this narrow road leading into the village for a couple of hours late yesterday afternoon. It was parked pretty much in line with the path out of the field, the route Kadi would have been forced along."

Forced, thought Mrs. Pollifax, trying not to think of Kadi being forced anywhere. "Do you have a description of it?"

He sighed. "Only that it was old. Used and shabby. Possibly an old army truck but too covered with dust to have color."

"Not very helpful."

"No, but at least we can—for the moment—assume she's no longer in this *immediate* area—that is, if the truck belonged to her abductor." His lips tightened as he considered this. "We begin a search next, yes. I'll ask Colonel Kapembwa for soldiers to begin searching down here in the south and work their way north. My police will start with Languka, a house-to-house search for Miss Hopkirk and for someone named Philimon, and for a truck of that description." He added politely, "We will find her, madam, we will find her."

Mrs. Pollifax thought it generous of him not to add "dead or alive."

When Inspector Banda returned her to the palace she was met by Joseph, who announced in a grave voice that her husband had telephoned her while she was gone. *Of course,* she thought, *to tell me on what day he'll be arriving.*

"What did you tell Cyrus?" she asked.

"You be out. You wish to call him now?"

"No—oh *no*," she said, and knowing that she couldn't bear to go to her room yet she turned and left the palace and walked up the boulevard. She walked the four miles to the airport, and after returning to the palace and only then, reluctantly, did

she enter the bedroom that she had been sharing
with Kadi, and where Kadi's luggage and clothes
were scattered everywhere.

That evening Dr. Merrick knocked on Mrs.
Pollifax's door and walked in carrying a tray. He
said, "Nobody saw you at dinner, and I caught a
glimpse of you this afternoon, and you looked awful." He pulled the small table over to the chair in
which she'd been sitting and placed the tray on it.
"You have here the miracle of one boiled egg," he
said cheerfully. "Plus one slice of home-baked
bread, one chicken breast, and one cup of hot tea.
And don't you dare tell me you're not hungry."

She smiled at him. "I'm not hungry."

He perched on the edge of her bed and shook his
head. "I'll force-feed you if necessary. Start with
the hot tea. *Now.*"

She lifted the cup to her lips and sipped.

"Good," he said. "I also bring you a sleeping pill
to help you sleep tonight. You're imagining the
worst?"

"Of course," she admitted.

"So let me point out one heartening detail, my
dear Mrs. P. Twenty-four hours—no, *twenty-five*
hours have now passed since Kadi was abducted,
and I can tell you with authority— Dr. Kasonde
will vouch for this—that each poor soul murdered

by the lion killer was discovered inside of *twelve hours*, if that's what you're imagining. Dr. Kasonde and I both agree that whoever this devil may be he *wants* his victims found quickly, for the terror of it, and kills accordingly. *Not* a new theory, I might add, dressed up especially for you. Inspector Banda reached that conclusion after the third death."

"I suppose that helps, but I was thinking of the attack in the garden on Kadi," she told him. "Which may be a very different matter, and a different person. You don't know Kadi's history in detail?" When he shook his head she described it. "It was only this winter that my husband and I prized more information out of her. She's done her best to blot out the day of her parents' murders."

"By Simoko's men called the Seketera, I've been told?"

"Yes. . . . She was returning to the clinic when she heard the gunshots, and hid and watched from the bush. But more alarming—since then she's confessed to me that she saw the face of one of the killers, and at the same time he turned and saw *her*, which makes her a witness, and dangerous to them if they're still alive."

"No, I didn't know that," Dr. Merrick said quietly. "Only that her parents had been killed in a village not far away. You feel the attacker in the garden could have been one of *those* three men?"

"It's been a worry to me from the beginning,"

she admitted. "Even before coming here. In fact it's why Cyrus and I felt that I must come with her, that one of the men could fear being identified by her."

"Hmmm," he murmured thoughtfully. "That *could* be important, Ubangiba being such a different place now, law and order having been established, courts and judges, et cetera. But, following through on that possibility, wouldn't this have to mean that one of those chaps has become so well-known and so respectable now that to be recognized as one of Simoko's hit men would ruin him?"

She gave him a quick glance. "That's very shrewd of you. It would certainly explain motivation this many years after the murders, wouldn't it?" She nodded. "Someone quite ordinary, living an inconspicuous and ordinary life, might not even know Kadi was here, and would scarcely be alarmed about her."

"But not," he emphasized, "if a man has a reputation to protect, guard, uphold, and sustain."

She thought about this with interest. "A man of reputation," she repeated. "Dr. Merrick, you've given me something graspable at last, and I thank you! Until this moment—a stranger here—I felt utterly helpless and useless." She nodded, satisfied, and began peeling the boiled egg. "I'll take the sleeping pill that you so kindly brought, and finish this dinner, because I see that I've a busy day ahead tomorrow."

Dr. Merrick grinned. "You don't care to tell me what doing?"

"I haven't the faintest idea yet," she admitted cheerfully, "but you've reminded me of something a doctor once told me when my children were small and given to collecting splinters and bits of glass in their knees that needed digging out."

Dr. Merrick looked amused. "And what did he tell you?"

"He said, 'Never bleed for the patient, let *him* do the bleeding, you just get the job done.' I've been very busy torturing myself over Kadi—bleeding, so to speak, for the patient—but now it's time to stop and get the job done. Using, of course, the experience I've accumulated from certain other dangerous situations," she added without explanation, and at once displayed her revived spirit by attacking her chicken breast with a knife, and so fiercely that Dr. Merrick looked at her with alarm.

15

Being unaccustomed to a sleeping pill, the effect of it carried Mrs. Pollifax beyond her usual eight o'clock; she woke at half past nine. Examining the world she would be reentering once she left her bed, she recalled a certain zest that had arrived with Dr. Merrick's late visit. After a good night's sleep she still pulsed with determination, but now she wondered how on earth she could use it to find Kadi when no one else could. She had told Sammat that as a *mzungu* she could see what others might not see but there were limits to this in a strange country. *Well,* she thought, *lying here in bed and thinking doesn't help.* It was time to nurse this small flame of resolution . . . visit Sharma, talk with Inspector Banda, and with Sammat . . . ask questions.

Quickly dressing she began her trip downstairs to fortify herself with whatever the cafeteria might offer at this late hour, but on reaching the second-floor balcony she was surprised to hear a hivelike buzz of angry voices below. Looking down into the huge lobby she was even more startled. This was not the usual mix of mothers and babies waiting to see a doctor but small groups of men talking among themselves, and with angry gestures. Working men with worn and dusty faces.

She thought in panic, *Is this how a coup begins, or a riot? Have they come for Sammat? Has there been a sixth death? What are they waiting for, and why?*

Behind her a door slammed and Sammat hurried toward her, followed by Joseph. "They've found the Lion Man," he said curtly. "The killer."

"And Kadi too?" she asked quickly.

"I don't know." To Joseph he said, "Take over, Joseph, I'll be back shortly. Mrs. Pollifax will come with me, they may have news of Kadi."

"But—whom did they find?" she asked as they rushed down the staircase.

"I don't know that either, Inspector Banda left an urgent message to come at once. A car's waiting."

Pointing to the men waiting she said dryly, "A phone call from Inspector Banda wasn't necessary for *them*."

"*Mfumo* Sammat," called out one man. "Who? *Ani? Ani?*"

"*Kaya*—I don't know," he called over his shoul-

der as he led her through and around them. "*Kaya!*
I go to learn."

They hurried outside to the car, where Bristol
Tanko was waiting for them in the Land Rover.
With a sunny smile for Mrs. Pollifax he said,
"Maybe Miss Kadi found, too?"

In the car Sammat explained. "What I do know
is that it was a busy night here in Languka. They
questioned every Philimon they could find, the police shone lights into every closed shop, and now
something has happened."

It was not far: passing Government House, they
drove through the gates into the police station's
compound, and here, too, clusters of men were
waiting. Mrs. Pollifax's heart began to beat faster.
As they climbed out of the Land Rover, the inspector came out to meet them. "They've found him,"
he said. "He should be here any minute."

"Found him?" repeated Sammat. "I thought—
already here?"

"The mask of a lion and a pair of claws were
what have been found here in Languka. Now we—
but here they come now," he said as a closed sedan
inched its way through the crowd at the gates and
drove into the compound.

The curious onlookers began to follow, until Inspector Banda called out sharply, "Back!" and to
Bristol, "Keep them out! Close the gate!"

The car came to a stop and the driver called out, "He be asleep in his father's *nyumba!*"

The rear door opened, and an armed policeman stepped out, reluctantly followed by a handcuffed man in a pale gray robe and sandals.

It was Dickson Zimba.

"Oh no," groaned Sammat. "Not Dickson!"

Zimba was frantic; he shouted to Sammat, "I am not guilty of this—*iai, iai*—no! *Ai ai ai! Bozda*—a lie!" He burst into tears and his glasses fell off, and the guard scornfully plucked them from the ground and pocketed them, not returning them.

Mrs. Pollifax said anxiously, "Kadi—Miss Hopkirk—*please*, you have her?"

Zimba only looked at her blankly, and with a nod to Inspector Banda the guards led him into the police station.

Sammat, stunned, said, "I don't understand. *Zimba?*" and to Inspector Banda, "Any sign of Kadi Hopkirk?"

Inspector Banda's stern face softened. "Nothing. No sign. It was Officer Chibabila who shone his flashlight through a window last night and saw a lion mask lying on a bed. We broke in, retrieved and tagged the whole outfit. It seems that Mr. Zimba rents a room here in the city behind the Bang-Bang Snack Bar, and this was his room. We were told that frequently he returns to the desert to

see his father, and that's where he was found. No—
there was no sign of Miss Hopkirk ever being in either place." With a brisk nod, he turned. "Now I
must question him, please."

Sammat called after him sternly, "No torture, Police Inspector!"

Turning at the door the inspector said, "No need
for it in any case, *Mfumo* Sammat, we have all the
evidence needed."

"But no Kadi," faltered Mrs. Pollifax.

"No," Sammat said in a broken voice.

It was unbearable to look into Sammat's face,
and useless to remind herself that she had warned
him of Zimba's burgeoning ego and need for attention. Useless because she too was shocked; who
could have believed it would actually be Dickson
Zimba? The reality of it was utterly different from
supposition or suspicion! In that one moment of his
defeat, leaving the car in handcuffs, he had been,
not a monster, but as vulnerable as any human being whose glasses fell off, and who wept—but over
what? the humiliation of being caught? the realiza-
tion, at last, of what he'd done? or the loss of whatever dreams had driven him to kill and mutilate
five people?

She grieved for Sammat and yet—in spite of the
shock and horror of its being Zimba—she recognized in herself a sense of relief; she'd been growing very afraid the killer might be Moses, that

scarred man whom prison and torture could have left erratic and unbalanced, and with whom she'd shared those brief moments of warmth. If it had been Moses, she thought—and she had to admit this—she would have felt pity. For Dickson Zimba, no.

She sighed. The killings would end now, but Kadi was still missing. If Kadi had not been found with Dickson Zimba, in either his rented city room or in the desert with his father, then it was possible that Zimba had nothing at all to do with her disappearance.

Which brought her to Philimon again.

Kadi had disappeared late Wednesday, and today was Saturday, and with each day—each *hour*—her disappearance was a deepening mystery, and increasingly ominous.

Sadly Sammat glanced at his watch. "I must go back—talk later with Dickson—now prepare a message to transmit by radio to the people, telling them the killer's been found. Tomorrow is Joseph's day off, his free day, and suddenly there is too *much* to do." He added in an anguished voice, "But why Dickson Zimba? My God, Mrs. Pollifax, five men killed and terrible rumors about me, *why? And where is Kadi?*"

She could only shake her head, finding no comfort for him.

Bristol drove them slowly back to the palace.

Tony Dahl was standing impatiently by the entrance. "Any news of Kadi?" he asked.

"Nothing," Mrs. Pollifax told him.

"Oh God," he said, and with a glance at his watch, "I've got two sub-chiefs patiently waiting for me, you'll tell me if—?"

"Of course."

He nodded and raced back to the farm.

The lobby had emptied. Sammat hurried to the staircase to return to his office and put words together for his radio announcement. Soon the talking drums would begin, she realized—but there was still no Kadi.

Mrs. Pollifax hesitated, and then she crossed the entrance hall and headed into the infirmary.

She found Rakia in the doctor's office rocking one of the AIDS babies and crooning to it. Mrs. Pollifax thought, _I could do this too once I've found Kadi, if only I can find her!_ After watching for a moment she whispered, "Rakia?"

Rakia looked up and nodded. "It's okay, he's asleep, I'll be back in a minute." She returned, sighing. "He will go to the bush hospital with the others, poor child. But Kadi, have you news, please?"

Mrs. Pollifax shook her head.

"I pray for her," Rakia said.

"Yes."

"Sit, Mrs. Pollifax, you look tired."

Mrs. Pollifax obligingly sat down. "Not tired, just very discouraged and worried. You're my last hope, Rakia, I need information. I don't know whether you've heard that it's possible Kadi left *willingly* with her captor?"

"Willingly!" Rakia looked shocked. "*Heya! Bani?* I mean, why? how? We've been so busy—smallpox and malaria and parasites—I hear nothing of *this!*"

Mrs. Pollifax said dryly, "Possibly because Inspector Banda doesn't *believe* she went willingly. They were all playing kick-the-ball that afternoon during the hour before dark, you see, and Kadi was over near the woods. The young man nearest saw her walk to the edge of the woods as if called there by someone. He heard her say—and he swears she said it in a *happy* voice—'Philimon, it's really you?' and when he looked again she was gone."

"A *happy* voice?" repeated Rakia in astonishment.

"The young man insists this was so."

"A trick!" gasped Rakia. "A *diva*—trap!"

"It sounds that way now," admitted Mrs. Pollifax.

"But this Philimon, who could that be?"

Mrs. Pollifax sighed. "The police and the soldiers have questioned every Philimon they could find in the villages down south and here in Languka. Now I come to you, Rakia. Because I think, and think, and *think* about how she sounded to this young man Jacob Bwanausi. *Happy.* Surprised, he said, and to sound surprised it must surely be someone she'd not seen in a long time, perhaps someone she knew back in the old days."

"In the old days," repeated Rakia wistfully. "Yes, that could be."

"So Rakia, I ask you: did she know anyone named Philimon back then? Did she perhaps go to school with someone by that name?"

Rakia said slowly, "There might have been a Philimon in the mission school, but I was nurse to Dr. Hopkirk in the clinic. There was a boy named Pharaoh, I remember. I knew many names of children but not all, no."

"Perhaps a friend to Dr. or Mrs. Hopkirk?"

Rakia looked puzzled.

"Think," pleaded Mrs. Pollifax. "Oh Rakia, think *hard.*"

"I am thinking." She frowned. "Police Inspector Tembo was good friend to Dr. Hopkirk. His name was Pharaoh, I think, but it could have been Philimon, it's a long time ago now, and anyway Dr. Hopkirk often called him just inspector."

Mrs. Pollifax said quickly, "Where can we find him? Where, Rakia?"

"Inspector Tembo?" She looked surprised. "Oh, he is dead, long since."

Tembo . . . Rakia was echoing something she'd heard before, and her memory was tugging at the name . . . something Inspector Banda had said; they had been in the garden, the inspector and Sammat, and he had said—but what?

"When did this inspector die?" she asked.

"Die?" Rakia's voice was harsh. "He be shot. So many killed! After the hunger riots President Chinyata kill kill kill."

It was coming back to her now: they had been talking about the strong room, and Inspector Banda had said, "In my entire life I've heard of only one person with such a gift"—at picking locks, wasn't it?—"and that was only a rumor."

But he, too, was dead. To find him, Inspector Banda had told Sammat, he would have to make sacrifices at the shrine.

"Yes," said Mrs. Pollifax and turned away, suddenly very thoughtful. Rising, she said quietly, "Thank you, Rakia."

She walked out into the marbled hall, past the waiting patients and up the staircase to the second floor and to Sammat's office. "Is he here?" she asked Joseph. "It's important, I must see him."

Sammat had said the other day that Joseph might disapprove of him for not hiring his cousin, but definitely, just now, it was Mrs. Pollifax of whom Joseph disapproved. "He be very sad," he told her reproachfully. "At Mr. Zimba."

"So am I," she said tartly, "but I must see him."

With a sigh he rose and knocked at the door of the inner office. When Sammat called "come in" she entered.

She found Sammat sitting idle in his chair and staring out of the window. When he saw her he turned his head away. "As you see, I am not writing my radio announcement."

"No."

"I have been wrong about Dickson Zimba, it is like a wound in me, but worst of all is no news of Kadi." He turned in his chair to look at her. "I feel helpless," he said. "To think of her—" He shuddered, and tears glistened in his eyes. "It is I who begged her to return here to Ubangiba and now— one way or another I can be destroyed, but not this way, not this way. What are rumors of sorcery compared to this?"

"I came to ask for the keys to the strong room," she told him.

"The strong room?" He looked blank.

"Yes. The records there, I want to see them again."

With a sigh he rose, and without question went to a wall safe next to his desk, dialed the combination, opened it and withdrew the set of keys. "Return only to me," he said in a dull voice.

Reaching the door she turned and saw that once again he was seated staring out of the window.

Sammat, too, she thought. *All of us.*

There was no guard at the door to the strong room on this trip. Mrs. Pollifax waited until no one was in sight before unlocking the hall door and slipping inside. Locking it behind her she turned on the overhead light, went to the gate of the vault, unlocked the enormous padlock, and entered.

Ignoring the files of the late President Simoko she went directly to the single line of drawers marked with the name of ex-President Chinyata. The British had taught him to keep careful records, Sammat had told her after glancing through them, and they had included fingerprints and photos of his police and army. A methodical man, Chinyata, in both his killing of dissenters and in his files. Turning to the police file she saw that it was arranged alphabetically, and impatiently she rifled through A, B, C, D, E until she reached T, her eyes moving quickly down the sheet of small photos.

And there was Police Inspector Philimon Tembo.

Her reaction was so violent that she quickly covered the page with one hand and looked over her shoulder, frightened lest someone be in the room with her and see what she was discovering. Because Police Inspector Tembo was not dead as everyone believed, he was very much alive.

Not dead.

"So that's it," she whispered.

She stared a long time at the photograph, but no longer seeing it because she was engaged in reappraising every event that she'd witnessed and every preconceived idea that she'd nurtured. She was astonished by this new dimension that she'd unearthed; it solved nothing and yet it changed everything.

When she left the vault and the room, carefully locking both gate and door behind her, several people passed her in the hall and greeted her but she neither saw nor heard them. Sharma had said, "You have already brushed against evil, but without recognizing it." He had also said, "There are watchers—and there are watchers."

After returning the keys she would go to see Sharma. She must.

16

Mrs. Pollifax unlocked her bicycle from the palace rack and set off down Government Road to the path that would take her to Sharma's. At the police station she saw a crowd of people milling around the gates; the words they were shouting were angry, and those in English were ominous: "Kill! . . . Murderer! . . . Beast! . . . Traitor!" She could only hope that Inspector Banda's men were prepared to cope with violence.

The well-worn path to Sharma's hut had been preempted by a family of guinea fowl, and it was necessary to keep sounding the trusty horn on her bicycle to gain passage. She thought they looked like plump and indignant matrons in pinstriped suits as they moved from the side of the path to its very center—"that's *ridiculous*," she told them, repeatedly sounding the horn until they made a final exodus into the brush. At first glance Sharma's compound was empty. She leaned her bicycle against a tree and called out, "Hello? Hello!" and walked up to the door and peered inside.

The girl Laraba came around the corner of the house behind her, a live chicken tucked under one arm. "Oh!" she said, and smiled. "The *mzungu!*"

Mrs. Pollifax smiled back at her. "Yes. . . . Is Sharma here?"

Laraba shook her head, and glancing beyond Mrs. Pollifax at her bicycle she said, "He have a bike, too, he's gone."

"Where can I find him? It's important."

"Oh well . . . he take a flat tire to bicycle repair. There is place next to Bang-Bang Snack Shop, with sign BIKES SOLD CHEEP."

"Moses?"

Laraba brightened. "You know? You maybe buy your bike there? That be—that *is*—where he will be."

It was by now midafternoon, and the overhead sun was searing. Mrs. Pollifax anchored her straw hat more securely on her head, thanked Laraba, rode back to Government Road, and turned up the boulevard. Ahead of her the road looked very long, shadeless, and hot, but she persevered, remembering that on her return there would be a tilt downhill to the palace. She was already anticipating the coolness of night when she reached Moses's gate and found it ajar. Dismounting, she pushed the gate open and wheeled her bike inside.

Moses was leaning over a bicycle in the center of his compound. Beside him stood Miss Verstoefel, the Swiss midwife from World Aid, and both were surrounded by a handful of small, barefooted black boys. There was, however, no Sharma.

She called out, "Moses? Is Sharma here? I'm looking for him."

Moses straightened and looked at her as if he had never seen her before.

Beaming, Miss Verstoefel called gaily, "I'm buying a bike! This red one!"

"Sharma come, Sharma go," Moses said gruffly.

"I see," murmured Mrs. Pollifax. "Know where or when I can find him?" Her glance drifted past him to a clothesline from which hung two pairs of blue jeans of different sizes.

"No . . . Sharma come, Sharma go," he repeated testily, seeing her eyes fixed with interest on his clothesline. "He be back early morning for new tire, is all I know."

She nodded. She was beginning to understand why she was not welcome, and turning away she wheeled her bicycle out of his compound, but as she rode back down the boulevard she knew that her visit had not been wasted, she had learned why Moses did not want her there, and this interested her very much.

It was five o'clock when she entered the cafeteria; she had missed breakfast completely and her lunch had consisted of a chocolate bar that she'd brought with her from home. It had been a busy day, and an emotional one.

She was hailed by Dr. Merrick, who called out cheerfully, "Chicken's not fried tonight, it's barbecued for a change. Did you hear Chief Sammat's announcement at four o'clock?"

"Oh dear no," she said. "Actually I forgot about it, I was busy trying to find Sharma, but without any luck."

"The speech was very moving," he told her. "A pity it turned out to be Dickson." He frowned. "I confess I never did *like* him. Pompous chap. Very insecure, but when people cover up their insecurities with arrogance it simply doesn't occur to them how unpopular they become. He'll find he had few friends." He looked at her. "You strike me as being hellishly tired. . . . Kadi, of course?"

"Kadi, yes," she said but added dryly, "a bit too much bicycling to and fro in the afternoon heat didn't help."

He nodded. "Probably one hundred degrees in the shade today. Word has it that Dickson Zimba's still claiming innocence, which, unfortunately, means that if he knows anything about Kadi he's not going to admit to that, either."

"No," said Mrs. Pollifax politely.

Watching her, Merrick said, "I've had a hard enough time with Tony Dahl rushing into the infirmary every hour on the hour to ask if there's news of Kadi. You really must eat more." Glancing up, he said, "Ah, Joseph, about to leave for your day off tomorrow?"

"Yes." Joseph was very formal. "I have message for Mrs. Pollifax." Removing a slip of paper from his pocket, he said, "It be from your husband. On his way, he say, and see you Monday morning airplane. Message came 3:10 Languka time."

Mrs. Pollifax thought, *He's coming too soon,* but she managed a smile and a thank-you to Joseph.

In his friendly voice Merrick was asking, "And what do you do with your days off, Joseph—sleep?"

"Oh no," Joseph said. *"Sleep?"* He looked affronted at the idea and said with dignity, "I have many books to study that *Mfumo* Sammat lend me. Accounting, and Roberts's *Rules,* taxes, and World Bank."

"Impressive!" commented Dr. Merrick, startled. "Not my idea of a day off—enjoy it if you can!"

"Yes, thank you," Joseph said, and left them.

Merrick looked at Mrs. Pollifax. "You're not exactly jumping with joy at news of your husband's arrival."

She said simply, "He's very fond of Kadi."

"I see, yes."

At that moment the drums began, the talking drums, and the few diners in the cafeteria were silenced, listening to that distant pulsating beat, so stirring to the senses. Mrs. Pollifax pictured its reverberations flowing with the winds to the south, where another drummer would send on its message west, until finally all of Ubangiba knew the lion killer had been found, and that rumors of sorcery had been false.

Merrick, studying her face, said, "You need a good sleep, Mrs. Pollifax, want another sleeping pill?"

She smiled at him. "Thank you, but no." What she needed, she knew, was time to think, time to sort out an overload of contradictions and confusions.

Excusing herself she went up to her room and lay down on her bed, listening to the distant drums and reflecting on what she needed to learn from Sharma. In the morning she would forgo bicycling and walk to Moses's bicycle shop, hoping to find Sharma there to pick up his repaired tire, or even better, encounter him on the way, which would save her a great deal of time.

17

In the morning Mrs. Pollifax was glad to find that her appetite had returned. She ate a hearty breakfast of porridge and eggs in the nearly empty cafeteria and set out on foot at half past eight, hoping that she might intercept Sharma on the boulevard. It was blessedly cool, and it seemed to her the boulevard pulsed with new life, as if the shock of Dickson Zimba's arrest had been followed by a profound relief that the dreadful murders had ended, the culprit was in prison, and their chief cleared of rumor. Violet Kamangu stopped to greet her and ask if there was any news yet of Kadi; Mr. Mbuzu, of GIFTS. FURNITURE, bowed and smiled; she was even acknowledged by Jim-Jim, the black-market dealer who said cheerfully, "No *mkambo*, eh?" and gave her a small secret smile.

The great wooden gate to the bicycle shop was closed; Mrs. Pollifax rang the bell and waited.

When there was no response she rang it again, but still it was not opened to her. She began pounding hard on the gate, then tugging again at the bell, and at last called out Moses's name. Peering through a minute crack in the wood she saw only a sun-scalded compound, but no Moses.

It was by now nine o'clock, and the shop was obviously closed—to herself, and to Sharma, and to anyone else—and she felt a rush of anger at this. Moses had *said* he expected Sharma in the morning; he had *said* this. Why, then, was he not here?

Baffled and frustrated she turned away, glanced through the windows of the snack shop next door—no Moses—and reluctantly walked back down the boulevard to see if Sharma was now at home, since he was not, after all, on his way to the bicycle shop. Turning into Government Road she made her way to the path leading to his home and walked across the fields toward the wood.

Reaching his compound she found it still cool from the night, the sun slanting through the trees and edging the leaves with gilt. She called out to Sharma, and then to Laraba, but there was no reply. She walked around the two thatched-roofed buildings and was greeted by chickens but no human voices and finally, exasperated, she sat down on the bench outside Sharma's house to wait.

A gray pigeon alighted on a nearby branch and then fluttered away; it was very quiet but she did not feel at all quiet, she felt abandoned, which was idiotic, but where, she wondered, had everyone gone? She had done a great deal of walking, all to no avail, and tomorrow Cyrus would arrive. *Thank heaven,* she thought, cheered by this, and then realized that since today was Sunday Cyrus must have reached Paris by this hour. She wondered if he had left word with Joseph at what hotel he'd be staying before his morning flight to Ubangiba, and then she remembered that it was Joseph's day off and she couldn't ask him. He might, of course, have left a memo on his desk; it was equally as possible that Cyrus might call *her* from Paris.

At this rate we'll miss connections still again, she realized. She decided to give up waiting and return to the palace. *If he calls from Paris,* she thought, *I will this time tell him about Kadi.*

When she had made her first visit to Sharma she remembered that she had been preceded by a young man in uniform who had left the compound—and Sharma—by way of a path running off to the south, whereas she had approached with her bicycle from Government Road. She thought that with luck the path would take her to the edge of the experimental farm that lay behind the palace, making it a pleasing shortcut. Definitely this was a frustrating morning: Moses's gate locked, with no Moses answering the ring of the bell, and now Sharma gone from his compound again.

She set off down the narrow path, grateful to the trees overhead that provided welcome shade. Soon the trees thinned, replaced by a virtual hedge of thick, high, leafless brush; this was annoying but presently she was even more annoyed when the path divided, giving her two to choose between. She stopped, weighing choices.

" 'Two roads diverged in a wood,' " she murmured, but in this case decided the more traveled path was the wiser, and she turned off to the right.

She had not walked far when she became aware of soft and cautious footsteps behind her. She stopped to listen, waiting for a friendly *"Moni!"* at any minute, but unfortunately when she stopped the soft pad of feet stopped, too. This was irritating. It also produced a feeling of dismay. She told herself there was no reason to feel uneasy; the Lion Man was safely imprisoned, but this brought her to the question of why the footsteps paused when she did, and why didn't this companion on the path hail her cheerfully, catch up with her and walk with her? It was useless to tell herself that she was foolish to feel nervous when her heart had begun pounding and she could feel beads of sweat forming on her forehead; impatiently she wiped them away with her sleeve. She thought, *I could go back and confront whoever it is, or I could start running, very fast,* but she knew that she would do neither, there was something important and puzzling happening here, and if instead she stepped out of the path and hid herself in the tall brush she could learn who was behind her, seemingly stalking her. *Stalking* . . . she shivered at the word.

With both hands she pried open a space for herself in the wall of wild scrub and vines and inserted herself among the thick and brittle branches. Silence followed, a heavy and oppressive silence, as if all the birds in the wood had been stilled, but no one came down the path, there was no one at all.

Until abruptly there came the sound of steps crashing through the forest of brush behind her. Not by the path, but behind her.

She turned, and screamed in terror.

He stood only four feet away from her, both hands lifted to kill, the fingers clothed in long, terrifyingly sharp claws, the face concealed behind a huge obscene mask of tawny fur with two slits for eyes, a ruff of pale wool crowning the lion's head, and that pair of carved wooden claws sharpened to knifepoint and poised to tear at her throat.

Not in prison—not—not, raced her thoughts, and then, *No screaming, fight. Fight, damn it,* fight.

She waited, eyes narrowed and concentrated only on those terrible claws. The man took a step closer, so close that she could hear now the heavy breathing behind the mask. Trembling, she steadied herself. Nerves taut, weight distributed, she made her first move, lashing out defensively at one of those two claw hands, blocking the one as his other fell to her shoulder, ripping the flesh of her shoulder and neck. The pain was excruciating but she refused it; steeling herself—it was her life now or his—she aimed a forward kick to his knee, which produced a small gasp from him, and in that half second of his hesitation her hand whipped out with a quick, hard karate slash to his solar plexus.

He fell back with a groan, tripped, and sank to the ground clutching his abdomen with his left claws, and from somewhere behind that obscene mask came the sound of retching. She watched, fascinated, as he lifted the right hand to his mouth and with his teeth savagely tore away the glove of claws, freeing the hand to begin fumbling among the folds of the dark cloak that he wore.

She stood rooted, dazed and bleeding, mesmerized by the sight of that one brown human hand emerging from those clawlike talons with its five groping human fingers; she marveled that he could still move after such a savage blow to his abdomen. She saw that it was a gun he was bringing out from under the cloak, and she watched this, too, with clinical detachment. Shakily he lifted the gun and aimed it. *Move,* she told herself—*move!*—but she stood frozen. The noise of the gun firing shocked her out of her unholy trance; the sound of it reverberated through the woods, flushing out a covey of birds that flew away in protest. She felt nothing. Instead it was the Lion Man's gun that spun out of his hand.

Bewildered, exhausted, and in shock she became aware of someone behind her and turned.

"Moses?" she faltered.

Moses broke through the underbrush and strode to her side, glanced briefly at her bloody shirt and continued past her to the man on the ground who was struggling feebly now to crawl away. Over his shoulder Moses said, "You know, don't you?"

"No," she whispered. "Nothing. Not yet. Who?"

He said, "Come. Take my pistol and keep him covered, he's still dangerous. I need to find his gun and cut off this mask."

She went to him and he handed her the pistol he'd carried. Dazed as she was, she felt no particular surprise at finding it was a 9mm Makarov pistol. Training it on the masked figure, she watched Moses find and pocket the man's gun, but when Moses leaned over him she closed her eyes out of dread, hearing him tear aside the dreadful mask. Only when he straightened did she open her eyes to see the face of the man who had tried to kill her.

It was Joseph.

"Oh, dear God," she whispered.

His face twisted in a grimace of pain, Joseph turned his head away from her.

Moses was bringing out a length of rope from his pocket. "Help me," he said.

She nodded, and when he lifted Joseph she was at least able to slide the rope under him, the blood from her bleeding shoulder falling drop by drop over Joseph's face, which struck her as so insanely appropriate that she didn't know whether to laugh or to cry.

Once Joseph was firmly trussed, Moses rose to his feet. Looking down at her from his great height, his scarred face was stern. "You're hurt. I've got to carry him. Can you make it to my truck?"

"I'm not going to faint this time," she told him with a wry smile, and with a glance at the pistol he'd given her to hold she said, "Would you like Kadi's pistol back now?"

His smile lit up his scarred dark face, but he didn't reply. Joseph had slipped into unconsciousness; Moses plucked him from the ground as if he were a child, slung him over his shoulder, and together they limped out of the woods, a sorry, bloody sight.

It was Roy Siwale, driving from Government House to the palace, who first noticed them: he saw Moses the bicycle man walking across the field carrying a man on his shoulder, followed by a white woman in a bloodstained shirt and then he saw that it was Mrs. Pollifax, dragging behind her what looked to be the head of a furry animal and he gasped, *"Heya!"*

Stopping the car he jumped out and raced across the field toward them. Behind him, at the Farmers Cooperative, a man came to the door and stood watching, and then he too rushed across the road. Two young women leaving the Milling Company office stopped in surprise, then strolled across the road to watch, followed by three small boys.

Seeing Roy run toward them Moses said, "Be firm. You and I take Joseph to the infirmary in *my* truck. This young man must tell Inspector Banda to come to the infirmary with guards."

She gave him a quick, curious glance. "You won't issue that order yourself?"

He looked down at her and said with a faint smile, "Who would listen to Moses the bicycle man?"

"Hah!" was Mrs. Pollifax's reply, and as Roy Siwale reached them she said, "We're taking this man to the infirmary in Moses's truck. Get Inspector Banda and tell him at once to come with guards, here is the Lion Man."

Roy stared at the furry mask and then at the man that Moses carried, and he looked aghast. "But this is Mr. Joseph Kamwi!"

Mrs. Pollifax summoned her most imperious voice. "We're taking him to the infirmary. We need help, we need the police!"

"But—I do not understand," protested Roy. "This is *Mfumo* Sammat's assistant!"

"Yes, and he tried to *kill* me!"

Moses, amused, finally spoke. "Mrs. Pollifax be hurt. You stand there gaping? Quick-quick! Help us," and bringing keys from his pocket he tossed them to Roy. "That be my truck, see? by Government House? Drive it here!"

Thoroughly alarmed, Roy sped away, and with a sigh Moses put down the trussed-up Joseph, whose eyes were open now. Mrs. Pollifax chose not to sit; she was not sure that she could rise again, and in any case there was a great deal to do before she could allow herself rest. She hoped that she had acquired her "second wind," certainly her dazed condition was being replaced by an infinite gratitude at still being alive. She took care, however, not to look at Joseph, whose eyes were blazing with hate.

Roy acquitted himself efficiently, Joseph was placed in the back of the truck and Mrs. Pollifax sat over him with the gun while Moses drove the short distance to the palace. With the battered old truck parked at its entrance Mrs. Pollifax handed the gun back to Moses and walked through the glass doors to find help.

Crossing the marbled floor she reached the door

to the infirmary and stood there, looking for a doctor. It was Rakia who saw her; she gave a cry of horror at sight of her and called out, "Dr. Kasonde! Dr. Merrick!"

"Mrs. Pollifax!" gasped Dr. Merrick, running down the aisle between the cots.

She leaned for strength against the door frame and said quickly, "In the truck outside. Please hurry, he tried to kill me. . . . Moses has him. . . . It's Joseph." And bringing up the lion mask that she'd dragged along with her she thrust it at him and sagged against the door.

Dr. Merrick dropped the mask, caught her and handed her to Dr. Kasonde. "Put her to bed," he said, and hurried off to see what she'd been talking about.

Mrs. Pollifax, rallying, called after him, "Don't let Moses get away, I need him!" and to Dr. Kasonde, "I can't stay, please just give me a bandage and stop the bleeding, there's more to do."

She was taken to a bed—it felt delicious but she had no intention of staying, nor would she lie down.

"But you need *rest*," Dr. Kasonde told her.

"Later," she said, as he cut away her shirt to examine and clean the wound.

In a shocked voice he said, "*Claw marks?* How is this? Who—"

"Sammat has to be told—it's Joseph."

"Did I hear you say Joseph tried to *kill* you?"

"He's the Lion Man," she said simply. "Not Dickson Zimba."

Dr. Kasonde's reaction was violent, and very American. He said, "Good God!" and to Rakia, "Tetanus, antibiotic, antiseptic, bandages, and— what's this?" he asked as he gently pried loose from the wound a necklace of bloody shells and feathers. Giving her a surprised glance, he added, "You had protection, Mrs. Pollifax, where did you get this?"

She had almost forgotten the necklace. "Sharma," she told him, adding softly as he worked, "When I told him I'd rather Kadi have it he said— strange, isn't it?—he said it would be I who would need it more."

"A very wise man," Dr. Kasonde said, nodding, and she winced as he injected a needle into her arm. "A fine *mlauli*, or prophet. You may perhaps prefer—" He looked up as Moses and Dr. Merrick carried Joseph past the bed and down the aisle. "You speak truth, Mrs. Pollifax, verily that is Joseph Kamwi. And I thought myself beyond surprises!"

"Yes, but are you through now?" she asked as he knotted the last bandage, and seeing Moses approach she told the doctor, "Inspector Banda will be coming soon. Moses has a truck, please tell the inspector—Sammat, too—that I'll be found at Moses's bicycle shop."

Dr. Kasonde gave big, shabby Moses a startled glance and said only, "But of course."

18

Leaving his truck outside in the street Moses grasped Mrs. Pollifax's undamaged arm, unlocked the padlock on his gate and they entered the bare compound, noon hot in the blazing sun. "Lean on me," he told her. "Lean hard." They walked past the awning-shaded workshop to the door of the little house where he unlocked this door, too, calling out, "Moses here!"

The door opened, and Mrs. Pollifax walked into a room whose dimness blinded her after the bright tropical sun outside. There was a small window in the rear; she could make out a chair, a table, another chair, a shabby couch— A figure seated reading on the couch leapt up and cried, "Emmyreed! Oh thank God, we were so afraid for you!" Racing toward her Kadi stopped, seeing the bloodied shirt and bandaged throat, and looked at Moses questioningly.

He nodded. "I follow Joseph. . . . Joseph followed *her*. And found her, but she is great fighter, Kadi. *And she knew you were here*."

Kadi burst into tears and flung herself at Mrs. Pollifax, narrowly avoiding her bandaged shoulder until Moses tactfully removed her. "Gently, gently, she's hurt," he said. He brought Mrs. Pollifax a chair and she was relieved to sit down.

Kadi's face was tearstained. "But to leave you, Emmyreed, to know how you'd worry! It was *awful*."

"And we *did* worry—terribly," Mrs. Pollifax told her, and her voice was unsteady, remembering. "It never occurred to us—or to me, until yesterday—that a mysterious man named Philimon could have kidnapped you—removed you—to save your life."

Kadi smiled. "I've cooked for him, and read his books, and he made a new drum for me, and we talked of the old days. But how did you know I was here?" she asked. "Philimon says you already guessed?"

"Because certain references to a Police Inspector Tembo, long since dead, began to interest me very much," said Mrs. Pollifax. "Because I made another trip to the strong room, and found his photograph in President Chinyata's old files and discovered that he was very much alive." There was a twinkle in her eye as she added, "And when I paid a call on Moses yesterday I noted a line of bright red on one of the pairs of blue jeans drying in the sun."

Kadi laughed. "Oh, I *wish* I could hug you! When I heard that Dickson Zimba was arrested—and Joseph still free, and nobody suspecting him—I was so worried. We were both afraid for you, I don't think you realized how vulnerable you were. Tell her, Philimon. . . . *You* knew."

Moses said gravely, "It was my fear that he'd plan to use you as bait—harm you—to bring Kadi out of hiding. He was desperate to find her, it must have been a great shock to him when Kadi returned to Ubangiba a week ago, he believed he would never see her again. Who knows what he feared? That she'd already recognized him, but was saying nothing yet? Or that at any minute a word, a gesture, would give him away and she'd remember him? From what Kadi has told me those three murderers never knew how much she saw that day."

"Just as Mrs. Pollifax pointed out," Kadi said sadly, "yet I would never have recognized him, I saw the face of only the one man, and it wasn't Joseph."

"But he didn't know this." To Mrs. Pollifax Moses said, "You have to understand how it was in those days. Hundreds were executed, but openly, in the public market. The shooting of Dr. and Mrs. Hopkirk was secret, hidden—a mystery—and they were revered, their lives touched everyone. People still curse their murderers and wonder who they were. If anyone learned that Joseph was one of the killers— you understand how dangerous Kadi has been for him!"

"But to become the Lion Man," said Mrs. Pollifax with a shudder. "*Not* studying accounting, or taxes, or the World Bank on his days off, but stalking people with those terrible claws. He must have gone mad. Utterly." She bit her lip. "Sorry. I must try to remember it's *over* now, except, of course, for Inspector Banda."

Moses, glancing out the window, said, "And here he is now, with *Mfumo* Sammat, who is looking *most* upset. We must go to meet them."

"But not Kadi, not immediately," urged Mrs. Pollifax. "One thing at a time! Poor Sammat has had so many shocks, and I suspect Inspector Banda is furious at having to come here, to a bicycle shop, to find me."

Her prediction proved to be right. As she advanced into the yard an angry Inspector Banda said curtly, "I would have expected you, Mrs. Pollifax, to come to the police station once you left the infirmary."

Sammat, glancing around the barren yard, said, "Or to me, to break the news to me—to tell me—" He closed his eyes to conceal his pain and when he opened them he had regained his composure. "What I don't understand is what you are doing *here*, of all places. They said you left the infirmary in a great hurry. And you are *hurt*."

Inspector Banda nodded. "My car is outside, we've come to drive you to my office, where you should have gone in the first place to make your statement!"

Mrs. Pollifax smiled at him benevolently. "In a few minutes, Inspector Banda, in a few minutes." Pointing, she said, "It's shaded over there under the awning, and there are benches. For myself I need to sit down—being *hurt*," she added with deliberate reproach.

She at once sat down, in effect forcing them to seat themselves on the opposite bench, while Moses stood protectively behind her.

Inspector Banda gave Moses an annoyed glance and said dismissively, "You can leave us now."

"Oh, no," she said pleasantly, "because the story you have to hear is Moses's story, and has been all along. You insist on standing, Moses?"

Moses looked amused. "Yayezz," he drawled.

"And no more of that dialect," she told him firmly, and to Inspector Banda, "His name is Philimon, you see."

"Philimon!" exclaimed the inspector. "This—*this* is the thief who stole Miss Hopkirk?"

"Scarcely," she said calmly. "He removed her from danger. Because, you see, as soon as he read in the newspaper about the attack on Kadi he knew there would be another." Not without a certain triumph, Mrs. Pollifax left her bench and walked around it to stand beside Moses. "He goes by another name now, but I'd like you to meet former Police Inspector Philimon Tembo."

Inspector Banda sighed. "Enough! This is ridiculous—impossible! Tembo is dead, and if this man pretends to be Tembo he's an outright impostor."

Sammat, frowning, said, "My father knew Inspector Tembo, but for myself I know only that he was very tall. This I remember, but I don't recognize this man."

Mrs. Pollifax smiled forgivingly. "Then perhaps the best witness to that is Kadi," and lifting her voice she called, "Kadi? Come join us now." And to Sammat, "Be kind, she is terribly apologetic about worrying us."

"She's *here*?" gasped Sammat.

"She's been here all the time, quite safe, thanks to Moses—or to Police Inspector Tembo!"

The door to Moses's house opened and a subdued Kadi walked out into the sunshine to say shyly, "Hello Sammat. I'm awfully sorry but you see, it was important." It was to Moses she went, reaching for his hand and holding it. "I heard what you said, Inspector Banda. None of you may have remembered Philimon but *I* did. He came often to see us, and once he made a drum for me that I loved dearly. He's made another for me now, while

I was here. We called him Philimon, and he was a *friend*." With spirit she added to the inspector, "And don't you dare call him an impostor!"

Moses looked down at her with affection.

"All right," said Inspector Banda, as if conceding the point reluctantly, and to Moses, "Just how did *you* know she was in danger?"

Moses pointed to Mrs. Pollifax. "It's she who reminded me Kadi might be in danger; she told me it was why she felt she must come to Ubangiba with Kadi. I had to think back—to remember. . . . Three men, I heard, three of Simoko's Witchfinders killed the Hopkirks, but the daughter had been smuggled out of the country. It saddened me when I heard of this. Suddenly last week the *Free Press* published news of an attack on Kadi in the palace garden, and then I *knew*." He looked squarely at Inspector Banda, his face kind. "Dr. Hopkirk was a man who cared. He taught my sons. We were friends, until— but that is another story."

Banda said, "Go on—Inspector."

"When I read in the newspaper how she'd been hurt I knew Mrs. Pollifax was right to worry, one of the men was still alive and Kadi had to be killed, it would happen again. I knew I had to learn the names of those three men in the Death Squad who murdered the Hopkirks, learn if they were alive and who they were."

Banda said sharply, "You mean you found their names?"

Moses nodded and drew a sheet of paper from his pocket and handed it to Inspector Banda. "The names," he said, "as you can see, are Mbuza Msonthi, Johnston Milingo—and Joseph Kamwi."

Inspector Banda was staring at the sheet in disbelief. "This is *government* paper, you could only have found this—is it possible?" Turning to Sammat, he said, "You remember my saying that I'd heard of only one man skilled in locks, Philimon Tembo?" And to Moses, "It was *you* who robbed the strong room?"

Mrs. Pollifax, remembering, gasped, "So *that's* why Joseph was so upset. *Not* the faithful, outraged assistant protecting his chief, but a man terrified at being identified as a Seketera. Remember, Sammat, how he wanted the culprit found *at once*, and—"

"Ordeal poison," Sammat said grimly. "Yes, he was as upset as I have ever seen him."

"But how did you know about the strong room?" Mrs. Pollifax asked Moses. "You told me you were in prison when the Hopkirks were killed, and that Chinyata was president when you went to prison. How could you know about the files, and where they were?"

Moses said dryly, "You are fortunate never to have been in prison, there is either solitary confinement or ten men in a cell six feet by six. And there is talk. Talk? It's all we had, but *that* is how I knew Chinyata's files had been moved to the new Simoko palace. For a little while—before they hung him—there was in my cell a young man who helped build the strong room for President Simoko. Poor devil, they couldn't let him live, he knew too much: where it was, the thickness of the walls, the iron gate, the locks. But I remembered, the details were written in my brain."

"And you survived, but how?" asked Inspector Banda.

Moses shrugged. "By accident."

"Nothing is by accident," said Mrs. Pollifax with humor, and received several startled glances; it was Kadi who gave her an appreciative glance.

"How?" demanded Inspector Banda. "Tembo was killed, yet here you are alive when everyone believed you dead."

Moses's smile was rueful. "And so I was. It did not feel good luck at the time." His fingers moved to touch the terrible scar across his face. "Philimon Tembo's number was Prisoner 186432, and Philimon Tembo was executed the second day he was in prison."

He speaks of him, thought Mrs. Pollifax, *as of another person.*

"A man named Moses Chona was 186452. . . .

Poor devil, I learned later he'd never been in the police, only been picked up at random in the riots. . . . I didn't know, nobody knew, but suddenly I was Moses Chona. Just one number different and I lived. And nobody noticed."

They were silent, thinking of this, until Mrs. Pollifax said with a frown, "But what I don't understand is *Joseph*. . . . He saved our lives last April, you know." Remembering, she said, "Mr. Lecler had a gun, he told us that none of us would leave the palace alive. We were *helpless*, Carstairs and all of us, and then Joseph hurled himself at the man and knocked him to the floor. He saved our *lives*."

Inspector Banda gave Sammat a sharp glance. "Joseph was only a servant in the palace at the time, was he not? And Simoko a harsh master. Is it not possible he thought *Mfumo* Sammat the better bet for his future?"

Sammat said bitterly, "And so I was, but I have been so blind! Am I still blind? Why? What did he *want*?"

Inspector Banda said dryly, "Perhaps your frugality shocked him. Also your integrity? You allowed no bribes, no corruption—"

"—or cousins hired," murmured Mrs. Pollifax.

"Living in luxury in a palace—even as a servant—may have spoiled him. And you turned

that palace into a hospital. A shock! If he succeeded in ousting you, is it not possible that he
hoped, dreamed of—"

"Of what?" asked Sammat.

"Of becoming another Simoko? Rich. Very rich.
And powerful."

Kadi said drearily, "Oh God, more Death
Squads, and already five deaths!"

Frowning, Mrs. Pollifax interrupted to say, "But
none of this explains why he suddenly pinned the
lion deaths on Dickson Zimba. Had he grown worried, even frightened? Moses, why are you shaking
your head?"

Moses said in a harsh voice, "Joseph frightened?
Never! You don't see it? Planting the mask and
claws in Dickson's room was a calculated risk, a
trick."

"Trick?" echoed Sammat.

"It gave him time." Moses lifted three fingers.
"In perhaps three days Zimba would have been
proven innocent, but three days gave him time.
What better way to bring Kadi out of hiding than to
place a copy of his mask in Zimba's room? Everyone relaxes. . . . Dickson is the Lion Man, Mrs.
Pollifax relaxes, perhaps grows careless, because
he assumes that she knows where Kadi is and will
lead him to her. If not—"

He hesitated; it was Inspector Banda who said,
"And if not?"

Moses sighed. "Once Kadi was safe I followed Joseph each evening. Two nights ago I watched him as he dug a grave out in the woods."

Startled, Mrs. Pollifax said, "Whose grave, Kadi's?"

He shook his head. "Yours, I think. Obviously he planned a death that had to be hidden. If you didn't lead him to Kadi—and you were showing no signs of knowing where she was—his only hope of bringing her out of hiding was to have you mysteriously disappear and *never* reappear. And by the time Kadi had been dealt with, and Sammat blamed for it, Sammat would have been lucky to flee the country before he was assassinated. And his accuser, Joseph, would have become the savior of Ubangiba."

There was silence and then Inspector Banda turned to Moses accusingly. "Why—once you guessed, and later when you knew—*why* didn't you bring the information to me? As a former police inspector—"

Moses interrupted him to say gently, "Please, what evidence could I bring you? I had no idea he was the Lion Man. Could I prove that he had tried to kill young Kadi in the palace garden? Could *you*? And would you have listened to Moses, the bicycle man?"

"You could have told me who you are."

"Were." Moses smiled faintly. "Philimon Tembo

died in prison, Inspector Banda, it is only among the five of us that I resurrect him. I am old, I am tired. I prefer to remain Moses. But to save the daughter of my dear friend Dr. Hopkirk—yes, I could still manage a little detective work. But I did it best *with no one knowing who I used to be*."

Inspector Banda said dryly, "Clumsy as I have been, I see that I need not fear for my job."

Moses's smile was broad. "From Moses? No worry, I give you all the success of it, and it was never the Lion Man I hunted down," he reminded him. "I was only after the man who killed my friends, the Hopkirks, and now wanted to kill their daughter." With rueful humor he added, "To learn the same man was the lion killer was a total accident, believe me."

"Still another accident?" said Mrs. Pollifax with a twinkle.

Banda's tense face relaxed for the moment. "And what did you so magically tell Miss Hopkirk to persuade her to go with you?"

Moses said simply, "That I knew who attacked her—it was Joseph. That he would try again to kill her, but no one would believe me. I could only say to her 'Trust me'—to hide her for a little time. To be safe."

"And I did trust him," put in Kadi, giving him a glowing smile.

Mrs. Pollifax said humorously, "But you should

never have hung her jeans on the line in your compound, the jeans she'd mended with bright red
wool loaned her by Rakia. It's true that I'd already
found your police photo in the Chinyata files, Moses, but until I saw those blue jeans—you were
selling a bike to Miss Verstoefel, do you remember?—until then I couldn't be sure, really sure, that
Kadi remained willingly with you."

"And that I was not the Lion Man," said Moses
gravely.

"All right, yes," she conceded.

"And I did not know, either—until today. Only
that Joseph was dangerous, and that once Kadi disappeared it was you he followed."

Mrs. Pollifax shivered. "I certainly felt watched."

Moses nodded. "While Kadi was safe in the infirmary I kept an eye on you when I could. I
felt—as I have said— that you could be in danger,
useful to Mr. Kamwi."

She remembered Sharma's saying, calmly,
"There are watchers—and there are watchers," and
she asked, "Was it you I felt watching me the first
time I visited Sharma?" When he nodded she said,
"And you followed me even after hiding Kadi in
your house?"

He shook his head. "Oh no, once she was safe it
was Joseph I followed, Joseph I watched. On his
free days and every evening, like two nights ago
when he dug a grave—"

"—and today."

"Yes." To Sammat he said, "She be one grand fighter, this lady, yayezz. She send him to ground—pow!"

"But Moses rescued me," she said, touching his hand. "Once Joseph reached for a gun I was so dazed, so tired, I couldn't bear to hurt him again."

Moses said stoutly, "He was dazed and tired, too, I do not think he could have hit anything except a tree, or maybe his own foot!"

She laughed. "Gallant Moses!"

Frowning, Kadi said, "What about the other two men, the men who killed my parents?"

"I have made inquiries," Moses told her. "Dead, both of them, under very strange circumstances, frankly. I would suspect that Joseph silenced them, just as he needed to silence you, Kadi."

Sammat stirred with a sigh and stood up. "It has been a terrible three weeks, but now that it's finished I am thinking of Dickson Zimba, who has suffered enough. Inspector Banda, we must see that he's released now."

The inspector nodded. "Yes, of course we must go, but I think we take Mrs. Pollifax with us," he said, looking at her closely, and with sympathy. "Dr. Kasonde said he gave her codeine for the pain, but I think she is in pain now."

"Only a little," she admitted, "but I'll go quietly."

"Of course Dickson will cry," Sammat said gloomily. "He'll weep on my shoulder again just as he did when I visited him in prison."

"Perhaps he'll have been sufficiently humbled now to be of more help to you," suggested Mrs. Pollifax.

Inspector Banda walked over to Moses and said gravely, "I will see you again, Inspector, I think I too have been a little humbled, I see that I can learn much from you, please."

"I will be here," Moses assured him with a smile.

19

All during that night the city of Languka celebrated. There was music, and the constant beat of drums, and dancing along the boulevard. Dr. Merrick, watching from the balcony of the palace, said, "If I were a psychiatrist I'd say that for the past ten months this country's been recovering from a nervous breakdown, a recovery interrupted by those hellish murders. I'd call tonight's festival a purification rite."

Kadi grinned. "You sound like Sharma."

"*He's* the psychiatrist," said Dr. Merrick. "Anxiety? Tension? Fear? He'll listen gravely to his client and then make an incision in his or her belly to let out the bad spirits, and sometimes—like this—there's dancing, shouting, the beating of drums. It's catharsis, and it astonishes me how often it works. All I'd be able to offer," he said ruefully, "is a tranquilizer pill."

They were interrupted by Tony Dahl, shouting, "I've been looking all over for you!" Waving a cablegram he said, "It's just come from Dr. Gibbons and it's *great* news."

Kadi, snatching the cable from him, read it and agreed excitedly, "Sammy has to see this, it really should cheer him up no end. C'mon, let's find him!"

It seemed that Dr. Gibbons was to return the next morning on the same plane as Cyrus: two of the artifacts from the dig had been found to date back to the fourteenth century; the remaining shards and objects were still in process of being cleaned and dated, but there was no doubt that Ubangiba had a promising archaeological site to be excavated.

"I think," Sammat said slowly, after reading the cable, "I think I can be interested in this now. Even, perhaps, excited."

Mrs. Pollifax said dryly, "And Dr. Gibbons can retrieve the trench coat that he left behind."

"And no doubt leave something else in its place," Tony said with a grin.

Sammat, looking ten years younger and his old self again, responded at once to Kadi's mischievous suggestion that Cyrus and Dr. Gibbons be met with a band. "Picadilly Popcorn Rock Band?" he said with a grin. "Sure, why not?"

And so it was that in the morning a larger than

usual welcoming committee lined up on the tarmac to meet the eleven o'clock plane. There was Dr. Kasonde—"to look after my two patients," he said. There was Judge Mutale, looking forward to meeting a fellow judge. There were Mrs. Pollifax and Kadi, Tony Dahl and Sammat, and lurking in the background Moses, who would soon vanish, guessed Mrs. Pollifax, being still shy and accustomed to remaining invisible, as he put it, but she knew where she could find him, and he would like Cyrus.

And of course there was the Picadilly Popcorn Rock Band, six young men in matching crimson blazers, white shirts, and black trousers. The music promised to be loud because they had set up an amplifier for their saxophones, guitars, and a multitude of drums of all sizes.

The plane began its descent, touched ground and came to a stop. The door opened and a stewardess appeared, followed by Dr. Gibbons, and then Cyrus, carrying a cane over one arm and waving away help from the stewardess as he began descending the steps.

"There's Cyrus!" cried Kadi joyfully, pointing.

"But he is tall," Sammat said in an awed voice. "Taller than I. Almost as tall as Moses."

Reaching the middle step Cyrus paused to look into the faces of the people waiting below him, and it was now that he saw Kadi with her left arm still

swathed in white gauze, and then he saw his wife
with a bandaged throat and her arm in a bright red
sling.

His comment was as pithy as only Cyrus could
make it, and loud enough to be overheard. He said
simply, "Good God!"

Whatever else he said was drowned out as the
Picadilly Popcorn Rock Band struck up a lively
rendition of "When the Saints Come Marching In,"
and at this Mrs. Pollifax felt a rush of emotion. It
was true that five men had been pitilessly sacrificed
to a madman's dream of wealth, but the nightmare
had ended at last and the man was behind bars.
There would be no more evil rumors of sorcery,
and no more lion killings, Sammat was still *mfumo*, Kadi was safe, and Ubangiba had its coal mine
and apparently a fourteenth-century burial ground.
Now, she thought, the country need only worry
about a poor harvest. Or the wells running dry. Or
an invasion of refugees from their warring neighbor. Or locusts. Or too much rain. Or drought.

But for the moment Ubangiba had returned to its
usual state of precarious normalcy.

And Cyrus had arrived.

LARGE PRINT EDITIONS

Look for these at your local bookstore

American Heart Association, *American Heart Association Cookbook, 5th Edition* (abridged)

Barbara Taylor Bradford, *Angel* (paper)

John Berendt, *Midnight in the Garden of Good and Evil* (paper)

Joe Claro, editor, *The Random House Large Print Book of Jokes and Anecdotes* (paper)

Michael Crichton, *Disclosure* (paper)

Michael Crichton, *The Lost World* (paper)

Michael Crichton, *Rising Sun*

E. L. Doctorow, *The Waterworks* (paper)

Dominick Dunne, *A Season in Purgatory*

Fannie Flagg, *Daisy Fay and the Miracle Man* (paper)

Fannie Flagg, *Fried Green Tomatoes at the Whistle Stop Cafe* (paper)

Ken Follett, *A Place Called Freedom* (paper)

Robert Fulghum, *From Beginning to End: The Rituals of Our Lives*

Robert Fulghum, *It Was on Fire When I Lay Down on It* (hardcover and paper)

Robert Fulghum, *Maybe (Maybe Not): Second Thoughts from a Secret Life*

Robert Fulghum, *Uh-Oh*

Gabriel García Márquez, *Of Love and Other Demons* (paper)

Martha Grimes, *The Horse You Came In On* (paper)

David Halberstam, *The Fifties* (2 volumes, paper)

Katharine Hepburn, *Me* (hardcover and paper)

P. D. James, *The Children of Men*

Pope John Paul II, *Crossing the Threshold of Hope*

(continued)

Pope John Paul II, *The Gospel of Life* (paper)
Dean Koontz, *Dark Rivers of the Heart* (paper)
Judith Krantz, *Lovers* (paper)
John le Carré, *Our Game* (paper)
Anne Morrow Lindbergh, *Gift from the Sea*
Cormac McCarthy, *The Crossing* (paper)
Audrey Meadows with Joe Daley, *Love, Alice* (paper)
James A. Michener, *Mexico* (paper)
James A. Michener, *Miracle in Seville* (paper)
James A. Michener, *Recessional* (paper)
James A. Michener, *The World Is My Home* (paper)
Richard North Patterson, *Degree of Guilt*
Luciano Pavarotti and William Wright, *Pavarotti: My World* (paper)
Louis Phillips, editor, *The Random House Large Print Treasury of Best-Loved Poems*
Colin Powell with Joseph E. Persico, *My American Journey* (paper)
Ruth Rendell, *Simisola* (paper)
Andy Rooney, *My War* (paper)
Margaret Truman, *Murder on the Potomac* (paper)
Anne Tyler, *Ladder of Years* (paper)
Anne Tyler, *Saint Maybe*
Phyllis A. Whitney, *Daughter of the Stars* (paper)

The New York Times Large Print Crossword Puzzles (paper)

Will Weng, editor, Volumes 1–3
Eugene T. Maleska, editor, Volumes 4–7
Eugene T. Maleska, editor, Omnibus Volume 1